"Hannah, are you okay?"

No. Please. Not him. Not now—anyone but him.

Hannah looked up and confirmed the deep, familiar voice was indeed Cody. She brushed her hair off her face and forced a smile. "I'm just a little overwhelmed by the pile of bills and junk mail today. You know how that goes."

Cody blinked rapidly. He moved closer and leaned in. "You seem upset?"

His dark brown hair smelled like a freshly cut Christmas tree. "I appreciate your concern, but I promise I'm fine."

"You're shaking. Do you want to go outside and get some air?" His eyes narrowed.

Fresh air. It was definitely what she needed, but not his company. She couldn't be rude, but Hannah didn't want her behavior to expose her secret. Telling Cody about that part of her life would create more panic. She'd seen the horrified look in others' eyes when she'd told the story of her loss. They couldn't imagine how anyone survived such a tragedy. Hannah often wondered that herself. She couldn't risk a panic attack in front of Cody.

Jill Weatherholt writes contemporary stories of love, faith and forgiveness. Raised in the suburbs of Washington, DC, she resides in North Carolina. She holds a degree in psychology from George Mason University, and paralegal certification from Duke University. Jill believes in enjoying every moment because God has everything under control. She loves connecting with readers at jillweatherholt.com.

Books by Jill Weatherholt

Love Inspired

Second Chance Romance
A Father for Bella
A Mother for His Twins
A Home for Her Daughter
A Dream of Family
Searching for Home

K-9 Companions

Their Inseparable Bond
Her Son's Faithful Companion
Guarding Her Christmas Secret

Visit the Author Profile page at LoveInspired.com.

Guarding Her Christmas Secret

JILL WEATHERHOLT

LOVE INSPIRED

INSPIRATIONAL ROMANCE

LOVE INSPIRED®
INSPIRATIONAL ROMANCE

Recycling programs for this product may not exist in your area.

ISBN-13: 978-1-335-93690-5

Guarding Her Christmas Secret

Love Inspired
22 Adelaide St. West, 41st Floor
Toronto, Ontario M5H 4E3, Canada
www.LoveInspired.com

Printed in Lithuania

MIX
Paper | Supporting responsible forestry
FSC® C021394

Who comforteth us in all our tribulation, that we
may be able to comfort them which are in any trouble,
by the comfort wherewith we ourselves
are comforted of God.
—*2 Corinthians* 1:4

To Jennifer for forty-four years
of friendship and laughter that all started
in Mrs. Preston's English class.

Chapter One

It was a mistake. That was the only explanation.

Cody Beckett's cowboy boots hit the fresh layer of snow coating the parking lot of Mountain View Academy, in Bluebell Canyon, Colorado. Hershey, his one-year-old German shepherd, barked before flopping down on her fluffy, down feather dog bed Cody kept in the back seat. "I'll be back as soon as I can, girl." Cody slammed the door of his extended-cab pickup truck and headed inside the school.

Stomping his feet on the rubber mat covering the tiled floor, he bent over and brushed the snow off his favorite pair of worn Levi's. During the car ride to the school, he played the voice-mail from the school secretary over in his mind. He removed his black Stetson and made his way to the principal's office. The aroma of Tater Tots from the school cafeteria filled the air. His stomach tightened with each step.

Five months had passed since he became guardian to his best friend's six-year-old twin girls. During that time, Cody witnessed no mean-spirited behavior from McKenzie or Madison. Now McKenzie had been in a fight on the playground—*no way*. Something wasn't adding up. This had to be a big misunderstanding.

"Mr. Beckett, thank you for coming so quickly."

The short, gray-haired woman stood from behind the L-shaped reception desk and scurried to Cody's side. "Can I get you some water while you wait? Principal Murray is finishing up a phone conference. Miss Simpson should be here with McKenzie any minute. Madison is helping Mrs. Fletcher, the librarian, shelf some books until you finish your meeting."

At six feet, four inches tall, Cody towered over the woman. "Water would be great, Mrs. Perkins." Cody's mouth felt about as dry as a three-minute egg long forgotten on the stove. With the upcoming Parents' Night on Friday, this wasn't how he wanted to meet the twins' teacher. He didn't know much about her, only that she'd recently moved to town to fill the vacant position.

Cody gripped the hat between his fingers and paced the floor until Mrs. Perkins returned with the water. He glanced at the picture window across the room. The snowfall had increased in intensity along with the wind, hiding the Rocky Mountains skyline.

"Here you go." Mrs. Perkins handed off the water before rushing back to the desk to answer the ringing phone. "Mondays always make me question why I haven't retired," she called out over her shoulder.

Cody unscrewed the lid. With one long gulp, he downed half the bottle.

Moments later from outside the office door, McKenzie's giggles echoed in the hall. Her mood certainly didn't sound like a child summoned to the principal's office.

Cody popped his head outside the door and spotted McKenzie. She skipped alongside an attractive brunette with shoulder-length hair that framed a heart-shaped face. Cody heard from the twins that their new teacher was young. They weren't kidding. Or maybe being forty-five makes everyone look young.

The teacher wore black, slim fit pants and a light pink sweater paired with black boots that hit below the knee. Despite the flat boots, she stood at least five feet, nine inches tall. The woman definitely didn't look like any of the teachers he had growing up in Whispering Slopes, Virginia. Holding McKenzie's hand while smiling down at her student, she looked more like a fashion model.

"Uncle Cody!" McKenzie raced toward Cody, all smiles. Her shoulder-length curls bounced. She wrapped her arms tight around his waist. "This is my new teacher, Miss Simpson. Isn't she pretty?" McKenzie stepped away, creating a private space for Cody and the teacher.

"It's nice to meet you, Mr. Beckett. I'm Hannah Simpson." A pink hue filled her cheeks as her delicate fingers reached for his.

"I only wish it was under better circumstances." Cody glanced down at McKenzie. "I'm not sure what happened today on the playground, but I can assure you, it won't happen again. Isn't that right, McKenzie?"

"Amber started it, but whatever." She shrugged her shoulders. "I'm just glad you're here to meet Miss Simpson."

Cody wasn't sure why McKenzie didn't seem bothered by the fact that she was about to meet with the principal. Something wasn't adding up. Maybe tonight he could get some information from her sister. Cody turned to Hannah. "I assume Amber and her folks will be in the meeting as well?"

Hannah nodded. "Her parents are on their way. The weather is delaying them by a few minutes."

Mrs. Perkins stood at the desk. "Excuse me, but Principal Murray emailed me. Her telephone conference with the school board is running longer than expected. You're welcome to use the smaller conference room, if you'd like. McKenzie can stay with me and color." Mrs. Perkins pointed to the large bulletin board on the wall decorated with drawings and colorful artwork created by the students. "She can make a contribution to our student art gallery."

"I want to draw a picture of Uncle Cody's dog." McKenzie looked up at her teacher and smiled.

"That sounds like a wonderful idea. What kind of dog is it?" Cody watched as Hannah took McKenzie's hand and guided her to the round walnut table in the corner of the office. Mrs. Perkins busied herself setting out the crayons, markers, colored pencils, and some paper.

"A German shepherd. Uncle Cody named her Hershey. He thinks she looks like a big chocolate candy bar since she's dark brown," McKenzie giggled before settling into the chair and reaching for the brown crayon and pencil.

"I'd like to see your picture when you're finished," Hannah said, flashing an endearing smile.

McKenzie nodded, already focused on her drawing.

"Shall we go have a seat in the conference room?" Hannah tipped her head toward the half-opened door.

"Sounds good. I'd like to hear what happened today. My guess is just typical playground mischief." Cody attempted to downplay the situation. He strolled casually inside the small room and hit the light switch. The fluorescent bulb overhead buzzed and flickered, casting a sterile glow over the room. He took a seat at the table.

Hannah followed him inside, her expression serious. She sat down across from Cody and squared her shoulders. "It wasn't exactly typical mischief, Mr. Beckett."

"Please call me Cody," he said.

Hannah nodded. "Since it's only you and I, you can call me Hannah."

"Will do. So what happened today?"

"McKenzie got into an altercation with Amber during recess."

Cody rubbed the back of his neck. He placed both hands on the table and clasped his fingers together. "Kids will be kids. I'm sure it was just a minor disagreement or something. McKenzie doesn't have a mean bone in her body."

Hannah folded her arms across her chest. A small grimace lined her lips. "McKenzie and Amber had a physical confrontation. Amber ended up with a scratch on her face, and McKenzie has a torn coat."

Cody shifted his weight in the chair. "Kids roughhouse sometimes. It's a part of growing up, right?" According to his father, Cody and his brothers—Luke, Jake and Logan—used to get into scuffles with classmates, but they turned out okay.

Hannah leaned forward, resting her hands on the table. "I understand children have conflicts, but physical aggression is not something we can ignore. It's important to determine the underlying reason behind her anger. We want McKenzie to learn ways to handle her emotions."

Cody shook his head, but remained quiet.

"You don't agree?" Hannah's eyebrows drew up on her forehead.

Cody released a long breath. "Look, I appreciate your concern. I know you're doing your job, but I don't want to blow this out of proportion. McKenzie's just a kid. I want her and Madison to enjoy their childhood. They've both been through so much in the past year. I don't think it's necessary to turn this into a big lesson. I can take care of this privately, at home."

Hannah's expression softened. "I've read the girls' file, so I'm aware they lost their father. It's tragic, but as McKenzie's legal guardian, it's important for you to guide her and set boundaries. Part of your responsibility is to teach her how to resolve conflicts peacefully and express her emotions appropriately. Fighting is never a solution."

Cody leaned back in his chair and crossed his arms. He considered Hannah's words. Raising children came naturally to his brothers. Much like how his younger brother, Luke, made being a popular bull rider appear easy. Cody's bull riding career was never as successful. Maybe he wasn't the right person to raise his best friend's kids? "I'm doing the best I can. McKenzie and Madison hardly know me. I want the girls to like me and to feel comfortable coming to me with their problems. We can handle this without making it a big deal."

"I understand you want to be their friend." Hannah softened her tone. "But it's important to find a balance between being a friend and a parent. As their teacher, I want them to like me too, but I must set boundaries. I believe we can work together to find a middle ground. I'd like to help you."

The knock on the door brought their discussion to an end—at least for now.

Mrs. Perkins peeked her head inside. "Principal Murray's telephone conference has concluded. She's in the larger conference room with Amber's parents whenever you're ready."

Cody pushed away from the table. His mind swirled with doubt. As they headed to the meeting, Hannah's concerned expression lingered in his mind. Was he capable of being the parent these girls needed? The weight of his responsibilities as McKenzie and Madison's legal guardian bore down on him, reminding him of the challenges that lay ahead. After the New Year, he'd face one of the biggest decisions in his life. Should he adopt the twins, or would they have a more promising future if raised by someone more capable? Cody took a deep breath and stepped into the conference room.

Wednesday after school, Hannah stepped inside the Bluebell Canyon post office. Two weeks earlier, she'd left Phoenix hoping for a fresh start and purchased a post office box. So far, the secrets from her past clung to her like gum on the bottom of a shoe.

During Hannah's first week of settling into her small, rented cottage just outside of town, a parade of neighbors stopped by to welcome her to town. No one came empty-handed. She had enough home-cooked meals and baked goods stocked in her freezer to last her until next Christmas—if she stayed that long. With an option to purchase, the home was a perfect choice to give her an opportunity to reinvent herself and hopefully bury her past.

The soft hum of conversations mixed with the clatter of packages being sorted in the back room filled the air. Hannah slipped her key inside the box and pulled out a stack of various sized envelopes.

She fingered through the pile of mostly bills and junk mail. Her hands froze. Wilma Simpson. Hannah's heart hammered against her chest at the sight of her mother-in-law's return address. The weight of the envelope hinted at something more than a letter or card.

"Hello, Miss Simpson." Ben Willis, the postmaster, threw up a hand. He smiled from across the room. "I hope you're doing well today. Let me know if you need any mailing supplies."

Barely hearing the portly gray-haired man, Hannah managed a weak smile in return. She staggered to the counter in a quiet corner. Her legs struggled to keep her upright. An uneasy dread seeped into her veins. She pulled her index finger through the envelope's seal. Three photographs escaped the folded letter that simply read, *I thought you'd enjoy these. Call me when you have time. Love, Wilma.* The photos fluttered onto the tiled floor.

Hannah's gaze fell upon the image of her deceased husband's warm and genuine smile, now scattered on the ground. Time slowed. Beside him stood their eight-year-old daughter, Jenna, once full of life. The child's smile radiated from the glossy colored print. Hannah had captured the moment of what would be their last family trip to the sandy beach of coastal Carolina. Rick's hometown and favorite vacation spot.

Emotions erupted like an active volcano. Hannah's surroundings closed in, feeling like a weighted, suffocating blanket. Her breath grew shallow. Panic squeezed her senses like a vise.

Not here. Not where everyone could see her.

She'd come to Bluebell Canyon to bury her past, not to have the townspeople take pity on her. The looks of pity were unbearable.

As grief threatened to pull her under and steal her last breath, Hannah scanned the room for a quick getaway. A restroom. Any place to hunker down until the panic attack passed. The post office, now a disorienting maze, made an escape impossible.

Her eyes welled with tears, blinding her to the other two photos on the floor. Yet she didn't care. Hannah didn't want any reminders of the past. It was the reason she'd crated all evidence of the family stolen from her in the horrific carbon monoxide incident. A once happy life now stuffed into twenty sealed boxes and stacked against the cinder block wall of her rental home. Unpacking them would only cause more pain.

Following the advice of her therapist, she inhaled several deep breaths to ground herself into the present. With great effort, she bent over, scooped the pictures between her fingers and crammed them into her purse, ready to make her escape.

"Hannah. Are you okay?"

No. Please. Not him. Not now—anyone but him.

Hannah looked up and confirmed the deep, familiar voice was indeed Cody. She brushed her hair off her face and forced a smile. "I'm just a little overwhelmed by the pile of bills and junk mail today. You know how that goes."

Cody blinked rapidly. He moved closer and leaned in. "You seem upset."

His dark brown hair smelled like a freshly cut Christmas tree. "I appreciate your concern, but I promise I'm fine."

"You're shaking. Do you want to go outside and get some air?" His eyes narrowed.

Fresh air. It was definitely what she needed, but not his company. She couldn't be rude, but Hannah didn't want her behavior to expose her secret. Telling Cody about that part of her life would create more panic. She'd seen the horrified look in others' eyes when she'd told the story of her loss. They couldn't imagine how anyone survived such a tragedy. Hannah often wondered that herself. She couldn't risk a panic attack in front of Cody. It could cost her the job that she'd grown to love. In the short time since filling the teaching position, being with the children filled a hole left in her heart. "That sounds good." Hannah adjusted her purse strap over her coat.

Outside, the frosty blast of air provided a welcome relief. Wispy, fair weather clouds meandered across the vibrant blue sky. "This feels good." Hannah took a deep breath while they walked with no particular destination.

"So you're a cold weather gal?" Cody slipped his hands into the back pocket of his jeans.

"It's not too bad if you dress properly." She needed to keep the focus off of her and what had happened in the post office. "Did you grow up in Bluebell Canyon?"

"No, I'm originally from the Shenandoah Valley in Virginia. My family moved here after inheriting some land."

"My best friend in college was from Virginia. It looks like a beautiful state." Hannah was relieved she'd been able to bounce back from the panic attack. Previous episodes often had lingering effects, particularly the ones that hit her in the middle of the night. They were the worst. A week following the death of her husband and daughter, Hannah experienced the first attack. She thought she was going to die.

"I love Bluebell Canyon, but Virginia will always be home." Cody stopped in his tracks. "Would you like to grab a cup of coffee? Sally makes a great brew."

"The Hummingbird Café—I love hummingbirds. I saw the place when I first moved to town. I've been meaning to pop in there."

"No time like the present. You can give me an update on McKenzie. You'll probably be too busy to discuss her classroom behavior on Friday at Parents' Night."

Hannah glanced at her watch. With no other plans and a half hour before a meeting at school, she nodded. "Let's go."

Cody scaled the front steps to the porch and opened the gate. Black wrought iron fencing surrounded the spacious covered patio area.

Hannah followed, admiring the quaint bistro tables.

"Since the sun is warm, if you'd like, we can sit outside. There are overhead heaters we can request to be turned on if it's too cold for you," Cody explained.

"Outside sounds nice." At times, being outdoors following a panic attack was better for her.

Cody pulled out a chair for Hannah. She settled in and tipped her face to the sky. "This feels great."

"I'll go inside and grab some coffee. How would you like yours?"

"Two sugars and two creams," Hannah answered.

"Sounds more like a milkshake to me." Cody laughed and headed inside.

Milkshake.

Hannah's husband always teased her about the way she liked to drink her coffee. He said it was like drinking a chocolate milkshake.

Despite the cold air, beads of sweat swept across Hannah's brow. Her heartbeat echoed in her eardrums.

Relax.

Breathe.

The sounds of passing cars and people moving along the

sidewalk amplified. Determined to ground herself, Hannah took slow and deep breaths. Her fingers quivered while she reached inside of her purse for a piece of peppermint gum. She ripped open the foil wrapper and raised the piece to her lips. A minty aroma wafted up her nose before she popped the gum into her mouth.

Hannah closed her eyes and kept her focus on the rhythmic motion of her jaw, allowing it to fill her mind with fond childhood memories. As a young girl, her mother would give her peppermint gum to settle her nerves before the first day of school, or when she got anxious about an upcoming test.

The coolness of the peppermint slowed her breaths while her muscles relaxed. *This one wasn't as bad*, she continued to tell herself until Cody returned carrying two cups of coffee in oversize foam cups.

"You'll never taste a better brew. Sally Raphine, the owner, is like a coffee bean magician." He offered the beverage along with a broad smile that brightened his hazel eyes.

Hannah discreetly slipped the chewed piece of gum back into the foil and tucked it into her purse to be thrown away later. She lifted the cup with both hands, allowing the heat to warm her palms. She inhaled before taking a drink. "It smells wonderful." She took a sip. "You're right. It's delicious."

Cody leaned in, clutching the sides of his cup. "So be honest, how has McKenzie been behaving in school the last few days?"

The last thing Hannah wanted to do was to steal Cody's gorgeous smile. Frankly, she was enjoying it way more than she should, but he asked for honesty. "She's had a few outbursts that have disrupted the classroom."

Cody's shoulders slumped. "She's been a bit of a handful at home, too. Since our meeting on Monday, I've made a point of asking her about her day at school. She never says anything, so I was hopeful things were better. Madison was tight-lipped when I asked her about McKenzie's behavior. I guess they work as a team."

"I think that's fairly common with twins." Hannah took a quick sip of her coffee. "I don't know many children who come home from school and confess they misbehaved."

"Why didn't you call me down to the school?"

"My mother was a single parent. I know it's difficult trying to juggle everything. Calling you to the school each time McKenzie acts out won't solve the problem."

Cody raked his hand through his thick brown hair. "Don't take this the wrong way, but before you took over as her teacher, none of this was happening. School was a place where she excelled. You can ask Mrs. Howard. She was McKenzie's teacher before she retired and you took over."

Hannah learned early in her career not to take things personally. By doing so, it helped to keep the lines of communication open between her and the parents. "Actually, I spoke with Mrs. Howard yesterday. I'm aware this behavior isn't normal for McKenzie."

"So what do we do?" Cody leaned back and sighed.

"We'll keep a close eye on her and continue to keep each other informed." Hannah reached inside her purse. She removed a pad of paper and pen to jot down her contact information. "Here's my cell number and email address. Please reach out with questions or concerns." She tore away the paper and slid it across the table.

Cody picked up the information. "Can I borrow a piece?"

Hannah passed the paper and waited while Cody wrote down his contact info.

"I hope I didn't offend you by my comment about McKenzie not acting out until you took over the class." He reached across the table with the piece of paper. "I wasn't casting blame on you. I'm just trying to figure out why the sudden change."

Hannah accepted the paper and tucked it inside her purse.

She looked up and smiled. "No offense taken. We're on the same team. I hope you'll remember that. I only want what's best for your daughter."

She couldn't miss the tightening in Cody's jaw. "Did I say something wrong?"

Cody shook his head. "No. It's just McKenzie and Madison aren't legally my daughters. I can't help but wonder if that's part of the reason McKenzie's behavior changed. After the New Year, the law will allow for me to file for adoption. Lately, I'm conflicted about my decision. Do you think McKenzie can sense it?" He looked up, maybe hoping for an answer.

Hannah nodded. "It's possible. Children can be quite perceptive. I don't want to pry, but would you like to share the story behind your becoming the girls' guardian?"

Cody took a swig of his coffee and placed the cup on the table. "Scott, their father, was my best friend. We grew up together in Virginia. After his parents died, we were like brothers since he didn't have any other family. He was happily married to Lisa. Out of the blue she'd become distant. Scott begged her to go to counseling, but she refused. She told Scott she was pregnant with his twins, but didn't want them because she'd fallen in love with someone else. Neither she nor her new partner wanted children. With the help of an attorney, Scott ended up paying her a large amount of money to carry the twins and turn over her parental rights. After the girls were born, Lisa signed the papers, but shortly after, she drowned in a boating accident. Life moved on. For almost six years, Scott and the girls were a happy family until he was crossing the street and was hit by a car. He suffered a severe head injury and passed away a week later."

Hannah could see the pain was still fresh for Cody. "I'm so sorry."

Cody nodded. "A year before the accident, he'd been preparing his will. He called to ask me if I would be the girls' guardian if something ever happened to him. When I agreed, I never imagined he'd be gone a year later. Maybe I was wrong to not take the position more seriously."

"Don't be so hard on yourself. Most people don't expect the worst will happen when making such arrangements." Hannah never dreamed when she left for her trip and said goodbye to her family, it would be the last time she'd ever see them.

"I want to honor Scott's wishes, but lately, I don't feel like I'm the most qualified person to raise the girls."

"McKenzie and Madison have both talked endlessly about your business training dogs. Maybe you could get them involved. It might be a way for you to establish a stronger bond and get to know them better."

"Funny, I discussed that very thing with my brothers the other day. We thought it was a good idea, too."

"It might help McKenzie channel some of her emotions in a positive way. She may find some solace and responsibility in caring for the dogs." Hannah glanced at her watch. "I hate to be rude, but I have a meeting at school." She fished in her bag, removed her wallet and laid a ten-dollar bill on the table.

Cody extended his hand across the table. "Your money's no good here. After all of your free advice—it's my treat."

"Thanks." Hannah grabbed her cup. "I guess I'll see you on Friday evening?"

"Right—the Parents' Night. I'll be there."

Hannah pushed away from the table. "Oh, I almost forgot to ask you. If you'd like, I'd love to have you come speak to the class about your work. Maybe bring a dog with you? The children would love it," Hannah said.

"Name the date and time—I'd be happy to visit."

"Is Monday morning at eleven o'clock too short of notice? The children usually have show-and-tell that day. I thought maybe I could surprise them with my show—a professional dog trainer."

Cody nodded. "You got it."

Hannah inhaled a deep breath. Cody had a big decision to make about the girls' future. He was a good man and certainly easy on the eyes. Maybe exchanging personal contact information wasn't such a great idea, but she wanted to help.

She shook away thoughts of Cody and scurried down the sidewalk for her meeting at the school. Afterward, she planned to contact the mayor's office to schedule an appointment to meet with him. Thanks to Nellie Garrison from the local mercantile, she'd learned the town was in need. If the mayor accepted her offer to take over as coordinator of the annual Christmas festival, Hannah could make a bigger contribution to the community. Maybe then she could put her past behind her and hopefully put a stop to the panic attacks.

Chapter Two

Saturday morning, Cody flipped the coffee maker to Start. It grumbled noisily before releasing its eye-opening aroma. He removed a box of cereal from the pantry along with bowls and his mug from the cabinet. McKenzie and Madison would be up any minute to watch cartoons just like he did when he was their age. If someone would have asked him six months ago if he could imagine himself raising two little girls on his own, he would have thought they'd gone bananas.

The sound of the two ceramic bowls clanking brought Hershey skidding into the room. Her tail swished back and forth. "I guess you're ready for your breakfast too, huh?" Since the twins came to live with Cody, Hershey had to learn to be more patient.

Cody placed the bowls and his mug aside and glanced at the clock on the microwave. Hannah would be here in less than two hours. Last evening at Parents' Night, he'd mentioned his plans to have the girls work with him in the kennel this morning. Once Hannah heard about Ellie, the latest rescue golden retriever in training, she asked if she could join them. "Come on, girl." Cody snapped his fingers.

Hershey hurried to the mudroom. Her toenails scratched across the hardwood floor. "After you eat your breakfast and the girls are up, we'll go out for a walk." Cody opened the twenty-pound bag of dog food and scooped two heaping servings into the bowl. Hershey buried her face in the food before Cody placed it on the tiled floor. "You're hungry. Let me get you some fresh water."

Cody filled Hershey's water bowl and placed it on the floor next to her food. "Enjoy." He scratched the top of her head, turned on his heel and headed back into the kitchen to retrieve his phone.

Moving through the quiet house, Cody went straight to the brewed coffee and poured himself a cup. He proceeded to scan and delete several junk emails. The device chimed a reminder.

Email Mayor Jennings.

Earlier in the week, Cody had slipped inside Garrison's Mercantile for a couple of Nellie's famous brownies. Nellie was always the first to know the news around town. While Cody munched on the warm brownie, she mentioned the mayor was looking to fill the spot of lead coordinator for the town's annual Christmas festival.

Cody considered the news. If he volunteered to take the reins, maybe it could be a way for him to give McKenzie and Madison a memorable Christmas. After losing their father, they needed to create new memories. If he got the twins involved with the planning, they could spend more quality time together. Hannah had already suggested having the twins help with the family business to create a bond with the girls.

Cody tapped out a quick email to the mayor with his offer to take over the planning. He hit Send, feeling confident about his decision. This could be the opportunity he'd prayed for. It might give him the confidence to move forward and legally adopt McKenzie and Madison.

Upstairs, the sound of tiny feet slapping against the hardwood floor warmed his heart. Cody had to admit, before McKenzie and Madison moved in, even with Hershey, the house had felt lonely. It was especially quiet after his ex-fiancée, Mallory, dumped him. Although they weren't living under the same roof, she spent most of her time at Cody's house. That was until she met the latest bull riding superstar, Billy Gainwell. Four months had passed since she hit the road to go on tour with him, leaving Cody heartbroken.

The girls stepped inside the kitchen wearing matching pajamas covered in tiny red hearts. Jake's wife, Olivia, had made sure the twins had plenty of clothes and shoes. He would have never survived the first few months of guardianship if it hadn't been for the support of his family.

"We're starving." McKenzie raced over to Hershey who'd gobbled down her breakfast and was now stretched out on her dog bed in the corner. With a full belly, she was ready for a nap. McKenzie dropped to the floor and buried her face into Hershey's thick coat. The dog ate up the attention and rolled over on her back for a belly rub.

Cody placed his palms on his hips. "Hey, where's my good morning?"

Madison ran to Cody and threw her arms around his waist. "Good morning! We didn't forget you," she giggled.

"That's better." Cody hugged Madison and kissed the top of her head. Poor Madison had finally gotten over the nightmares she experienced from losing her father.

McKenzie jumped to her feet and repeated her sister's actions. "Sorry, but I've always wanted my own dog."

"Well, now you have one. Hershey is part of our family." Cody bent and wrapped his arms around McKenzie.

"But we're not a real family." McKenzie crinkled her nose and pushed the wild, tousled curls away from her face.

"Don't say that!" Madison cried.

McKenzie's face scrunched up. "What? It's true—even Jodi at school said so. Uncle Cody isn't a real uncle. He was Daddy's best friend."

Cody's stomach twisted. Had similar comments by the

other students been the reason McKenzie continued to act out at school?

Madison moved closer to Cody. "But he's our guardian. That's kind of the same as family, isn't it?" She gazed up at him. Confusion filled her brown eyes.

Cody smiled down at the twins. "I might not be your real uncle by blood, but that doesn't mean we're not family. Love makes a family—not only blood. I hope you'll both remember that."

"I will. Jodi doesn't know what she's talking about." Madison nuzzled her face into Cody's hip and squeezed tight.

McKenzie didn't respond. This was no surprise to Cody. She had never shared her feelings about losing her father. Unlike Madison, McKenzie had shed no tears—at least not in front of him. The counselor had insisted this was normal. McKenzie had assumed the role of her sister's protector.

"Can we take Hershey for a walk after breakfast?" McKenzie flopped down in the chair at the kitchen table.

"That's the plan. I also thought maybe you would like to help me with Ellie today."

Madison jumped up and down. "The new puppy?"

Cody kept a close eye on McKenzie. He hoped she'd be excited about the idea. "Yes. Ellie is the golden retriever your uncle Logan rescued a couple of weeks ago. If you'd like, we can do a little leash training."

Still no reaction from McKenzie, but Madison seemed up for the idea.

Fearing a negative reaction, Cody wasn't sure if he should tell the twins Hannah planned to join them today. But then again, it might be better to deal with any opposition before Hannah arrived. "I've invited Miss Simpson over to help."

McKenzie's eyes widened. She flew out of the chair and ran to Cody. "Our teacher? Really? Is she coming because of what happened with Amber?" McKenzie glanced at her sister, bouncing up and down on her toes.

Madison stood with her hands behind her back, wearing a pasted-on smile.

Strange. Why would McKenzie get excited about the possibility of her teacher coming over because of the trouble she'd gotten into with Amber? "Yes, Miss Simpson is visiting, but I invited her after she showed some interest in dogs."

McKenzie and Madison giggled and exchanged looks. Both shrugged their shoulders.

"It doesn't matter why. At least she's coming." McKenzie's face beamed like a bright star in an inky sky. They grabbed each other's hand and ran in circles around the kitchen, dancing and twirling.

Cody shook his head. He wasn't sure what was going on with them. Maybe it was a twin thing.

After breakfast, without instruction, the girls went upstairs to brush their teeth and get ready for the walk. Cody had heard more giggles and whispering while he cleaned up the kitchen. When Cody was their age, he couldn't imagine being excited to have his teacher come to his home.

Outside, following a short hike, the three rounded the path that circled the pond on Logan's property for the second time. Hershey barked at a flock of geese gliding on the water. Donald, the resident Muscovy duck, waddled along the water's edge, but didn't seem phased by Hershey.

McKenzie and Madison wore jeans and their yellow thermal coats while Cody stuck with his flannel hoodie. He loved the weather this time of the year. The morning air carried an invigorating chill. But with sunshine and a calm wind in the forecast, the temperature would only go up. "We better head back to the house. Miss Simpson should be here any minute."

McKenzie wore a huge grin as she reached for Hershey's leash. She bounced in her sneakers. "We can keep walking

Hershey if you want to talk alone with Miss Simpson." Both girls giggled, barely able to contain their excitement.

What was up with these two? "No, we can all welcome your teacher. There's no reason for me to speak to her alone."

Minutes later, back at the house, Cody settled into the rocking chair on the sturdy oak front porch. The space was exactly what he'd had in mind when he and the builder designed the home. Both inviting and offering a picturesque view of the Colorado Rockies, along with the vast rolling meadow.

"She's here! She's here!" The girls ran across the front yard, whooping and flailing their arms overhead. Hershey barked while chasing their heels.

Cody stood and wiped his palms down the front of his jeans. His heartbeat quickened when he spotted a white SUV heading up the gravel driveway. Why was he so nervous? Or was he just as excited as the twins to spend time with their teacher?

Hannah parked the vehicle and exited. Dark-wash jeans and a short, well-fitted down jacket accentuated her slim figure. Paired with western boots and a brown cowboy hat, Hannah looked as though she was born for ranch life.

McKenzie and Madison ran to greet their teacher.

Cody waved and crossed the grass. "Welcome to the ranch." He tipped his Stetson. "The girls have been bursting with excitement since I told them you were coming to help with Ellie."

Hannah smiled at the girls. "Thank you for inviting me." She scanned the property. "It's so beautiful here."

"Thank you." Hannah's presence definitely added to the beauty. "You look great," Cody said.

Hannah's cheeks turned pink. She gazed at the ground. "Thanks."

"I didn't mean to embarrass you. I meant to say you fit right in on the ranch with your outfit and all." Cody's face heated up. "Maybe I should just keep quiet," he said, smiling.

"If you want, you guys can walk alone to the paddock," McKenzie suggested.

Cody arched a brow at Hannah before turning his attention back to McKenzie. "No we'll all go together." Cody glanced at Hannah. "Would you like a tumbler of coffee to take along?"

"No, thank you. I had my two cups earlier this morning. That's usually my limit."

"Okay, that's settled. Let's all go together." Cody whistled for Hershey to join them.

"See you there!" Like a disturbed swarm of bees, McKenzie grabbed her sister's hand. They took off running through the grassy meadow.

"Come on Hershey," Madison commanded.

Hershey, no longer leashed, looked to Cody. "Go on." He pointed in the girls' direction. The animal ran to catch up.

Hannah and Cody walked alone—exactly how the girls seemed to want them to be since Hannah arrived. At least that was Cody's instinct.

"The girls seem excited to see Ellie. I'm a little eager myself. What you and your brothers do is admirable."

Cody slowed his pace and glanced at Hannah. "You're familiar with Beckett's Canine Training?"

Hannah's eye shifted in his direction. "I confess, after you invited me to join you today, I did a little internet research. You and your brothers have made a name for yourselves in this part of the country."

"We're blessed to do what we love. So you're a dog lover?" Cody couldn't imagine anyone not liking dogs.

"You could say that. I've always had a soft spot for animals, particularly the rescues. We—I mean, I thought about getting a dog, but with my busy schedule, I don't think it would be fair to the animal."

Cody couldn't miss the change in Hannah's tone when she corrected herself after she'd misspoken. Unlike her having access to school records, he wasn't able to read a file about her background. Was she still a *we* or maybe she'd been dumped by her fiancé too? Of course, it wasn't his place to ask. But the day was only getting started. Who knew what he might learn about the lovely Hannah Simpson?

Despite the puffs of vapor escaping Hannah's lips, warmth filled her body while hiking along Logan's property. While she and Cody scaled the rolling hills, she continued to convince herself it wasn't the company creating the warm and fuzzy feeling. It had to be the hills—right? But she always set her treadmill on a steep incline. There was no denying the fact. Cody was undoubtedly the first man she'd found attractive since meeting her husband.

"Girls, didn't I tell you to always keep the gate shut?"

Cody's question broke into her thoughts—probably a good thing.

"Madison came in behind me," McKenzie yelled from across the paddock.

"Sorry. I forgot." Madison ran and took a place beside her sister outside of the locked door of the climate-controlled kennel.

"Okay, just try to remember next time." Cody slipped a plastic pass card and swiped it across the electronic keypad.

Hannah took in the elaborate structure. From the outside it resembled a large barn, but along with the traditional rustic wood, the roof was steeply pitched and constructed of steel and tin. Large windows lined the front. "This place looks incredible. I've seen a few dog kennels, but nothing like this."

"Wait until you see the inside!" McKenzie grabbed her teacher's hand.

Cody smiled at Hannah before opening the door.

Hannah stepped inside, and her mouth dropped open. "This is absolutely amazing. It's even bigger than it looks from the outside." The soaring high ceiling and exposed wooden beams caught her attention. "I want to live here."

McKenzie and Madison giggled.

"It's so quiet. I can't believe there are other dogs here besides Ellie." Hannah looked toward the spacious cages lining the wall across from the front entrance.

"That's because they're all trained. Right, Uncle Cody?" Madison smiled.

Cody slipped his hands into the back pockets of his jeans. "That's true, but that doesn't mean things don't get rowdy in here sometimes. The animals currently housed are further along with their training. We have a separate area for the newly rescued."

The girls and Hershey went to visit with a few of the dogs. Hannah followed Cody as he moved across the facility. "I think I remember reading in one of the online articles about the puppy raiser camp. That sounds like fun."

Cody nodded. "Jake, my older brother, runs the camp on his property. He loves it. But this training area is all thanks to my younger brother, Logan. It was his dream to establish a dog rescue organization. Last year, we rebuilt and expanded this facility. We wanted to make sure our animals have the best environment possible. We specifically designed everything for the dogs' comfort and safety."

Hannah admired the expansive interior, which was divided into multiple training areas. The natural light filling the room made the space bright and inviting.

"The padded flooring is perfect for some of our rigorous training sessions. Plus, it's good for my aging knees," Cody laughed.

They continued working their way through the structure and rounded a corner.

"Here's Ellie's condo." Cody winked and stopped in front of the kennel.

Hannah's insides vibrated while she patiently waited for Cody to unlock the cage. Ellie yipped and jumped, longing to be free from the confined space.

"Hold on, girl." Cody slid the door open. Once free, Ellie ran straight to Hannah.

Hannah dropped to the floor. "She's the most adorable puppy I've ever seen." She buried her face in the golden fur. Ellie wiggled and squirmed with excitement. "I think I'm in love," Hannah sang.

"It looks like the feeling is mutual," Cody said, smiling.

"How old is she?" Given Ellie's size, Hannah wouldn't refer to her as a puppy.

Cody reached for a leather leash hanging on a nearby hook. "She's a year old, big for a puppy, right?"

"That's exactly what I was thinking."

"She might look it, but she's not fully matured. Aren't you, girl?" Cody patted her flank and attached the leash to her collar. "The weather outside is perfect for a little leash training. Girls, come on. Let's go." Cody motioned for McKenzie and Madison.

Outside, brilliant sunshine in the clear sky provided enough warmth for Hannah to shed her winter coat. She flung it over the edge of the split rail fencing lined with wiring.

Ellie bounced with excitement. The leash remained taut as Cody maintained a gentle hold.

Hannah walked alongside and observed Cody effortlessly leading Ellie around the paddock. The dog's ears perked at the birds chirping in the trees. "Why is leash training so important? Isn't that something that comes naturally?"

Cody's eyes brightened. "You would think so, wouldn't you? Walking patiently while leashed is necessary in order to establish a bond between the dog and its handler. The connection will help Ellie learn to trust and follow commands."

"I imagine the training helps to keep Ellie safe as well."

"You're pretty smart." Cody winked. "I guess that's what makes you a brilliant teacher."

Hannah's face warmed. "That's kind of you to say, but I haven't been in town long enough to prove myself."

"I don't know. It seems you've done a good job so far." Cody paused and inhaled a noticeably quick breath. "But, you're right. The leash training gives me control over Ellie's movements, particularly in a dangerous situation."

"Like if a wild animal comes around?" McKenzie, who'd been quietly observing with her sister, chimed in.

"You're exactly correct. The leash prevents her from running off and possibly getting seriously injured. The primary goal is to teach the dog to walk calmly with its handler and not to pull on the leash. We want Ellie to exhibit good behavior both inside and outside of the kennel."

Cody handed off the leather strap to Hannah. "Here, you take over."

Hannah gripped the leash. "What do I do now?" Her palms moistened with sweat. Cody trusted her with Ellie. She didn't want to disappoint him.

Cody grinned. "Just start walking with her. Remember to keep the leash loose so Ellie feels comfortable and senses you're relaxed."

Hannah took a few steps, but Ellie was eager to move faster. The dog tugged hard, almost jerking the leash from Hannah's hand. Her eyes shot to Cody for help.

"It's okay. Just give a slight tug on the leash and tell her *no*. It will let her know it's time for her to listen to your command."

Hannah followed Cody's instructions. With one small pull, Ellie stopped. Almost simultaneously, the dog looked back in Hannah's direction.

"You're a natural." Cody moved closer to Hannah. "Ellie feels she can trust you. You're forming that bond with her."

A lightness filled Hannah's chest. Feeling a connection,

she had a longing to spend more time working with Ellie. "I don't want to come across as too forward, but I'd love to volunteer to help you work with Ellie."

"Yay! Can she, Uncle Cody?" McKenzie called out.

"My brothers and I always welcome volunteers. Are you sure you have the time?"

Spending time with Ellie was the most at peace Hannah remembered feeling in a long time. Perhaps it could help control the panic attacks? So far, she loved Bluebell Canyon and her job. She didn't want an attack while at school to jeopardize her teaching position. "I definitely have the time. I'd love to help in any way I can."

Cody extended his hand. "Welcome aboard."

They shook hands. The girls whooped and jumped up and down. Ellie and Hershey barked.

"With your help, Ellie might be ready for her handler sooner than I planned," Cody said.

"Do you have someone in mind?" Hannah resumed her walk with the dog.

Cody strolled with Hannah. "Not yet, but my brothers and I are confident we'll find a person in need of a psychiatric service dog. Sadly, there are far too many people suffering in silence with PTSD and panic attacks."

Hannah stopped abruptly in her tracks. Ellie jerked hard on the leash, struggling to break free. Did Ellie sense the apprehension coursing through her body? Hannah couldn't volunteer to help Cody train a dog to respond to panic attacks. Not when it was crucial for her attacks to remain a secret.

Chapter Three

Early on Monday, Cody put the last cereal bowl into the dishwasher and powered it on.

Olivia had stopped by to drive the girls to school. The house was quiet.

"Just like old times, right Hershey?" He looked down at the animal.

Hershey jumped to her feet. She circled him three times with her let's-go-for-a-walk move.

Cody glanced at his watch. He had plenty of time before he and Ellie were due at the school. "Okay, let me grab your leash."

Outside, thanks to the brilliant sunshine, the light dusting of snow that had fallen overnight had already disappeared. Cody inhaled the invigorating crisp, cold air into his lungs. *Better than caffeine.* As though on autopilot, with her nose to the ground, Hershey headed toward the pond on Logan's property. Cody allowed her to lead the way.

As they neared the top of the hill, Logan appeared from behind a group of pine trees.

"Hey, buddy. Do you mind if I join you?" Logan asked.

"Sure, we're just headed to the pond for a walk. Are you looking for your Christmas tree?" Cody laughed. On his list of things to do was to find the biggest tree he could for McKenzie and Madison.

Logan adjusted his Stetson as they moved through the grassy meadow. "Actually, I was. Henry was quizzing me about the tree last night, so Caitlyn thought it was time. She even had me go up into the attic and bring down some of the boxes of decorations."

It thrilled Cody to see his younger brother so happy. Logan adopted Henry after he and Caitlyn married. His brother stepped up to the plate and made fatherhood look like he'd been doing it for years. A part of Cody longed for the same, but the twins had experienced a lot of change already. What if he wasn't cut out for single fatherhood? The last thing Cody wanted to do was cause them more pain and heartache.

"Jake told me you're taking Ellie to the school this morning."

"That's right. The twins' teacher invited me to do a presentation. She thought the class would enjoy hearing about our work and meeting a dog in training." Cody and his brothers had visited many schools around the state. It was important to make those in need, along with their families, aware of the options for service dogs and their benefits.

"I like the way she thinks. The more schools we can visit, the better. Do you need any help this morning?"

"Thanks for the offer, but since I'm only taking Ellie, I can manage."

"So what's the teacher like?" Logan nudged Cody's arm. "I haven't met her yet, but I hear she's easy on the eyes."

Cody released a long breath as they completed the first circle around the pond. *Here we go again.* It wasn't long after his fiancée walked out that his brothers started playing matchmaker. No matter how much Cody tried to convince his family he was okay with being alone, they weren't buying it. His sisters-in-law were even more adamant about finding him a wife. If they had their way, he would be married by the end of the year. Cody understood they only wanted him to be happy, so he did his best to overlook their persistent ways. "Hannah is nice."

Logan laughed. "Nice? Come on now. Caitlyn told me that Olivia said she spent Saturday morning with you and the girls."

"Sometimes I think my brothers' wives have cameras around my property," Cody joked. "Hannah came over to meet Ellie. She's actually going to help me train her."

"Oh, is she now?" Logan's brow arched.

Cody ignored Logan's sarcastic tone. "Well, I think she is."

"What does that mean?"

"It was kind of strange. Hannah loved Ellie. It surprised me when she offered to volunteer her time to help train Ellie, given her busy schedule at the school. But then suddenly it seemed she wanted to take back her offer." Cody hadn't been able to shake the uneasy feeling that he'd done something to make her change her mind.

"That doesn't make any sense. Why would she put the offer out there in the first place?" Logan shook his head.

"Once I mentioned Ellie being trained to assist handlers who have PTSD and panic attacks, she seemed to shut down. She left shortly after. Even the twins noticed something different about her. McKenzie got an attitude with me and said I must have done or said something to make their teacher mad."

Logan shrugged his shoulders. "I suppose she'll let you know if she changed her mind."

"True. Once I'm finished with the presentation at the school, I plan to ask her which days she's available to work with Ellie. If she's having reservations, I'm sure she'll let me know."

"Sounds like a plan. Good luck, brother."

Later that morning, Cody and Ellie stood on the stage of the auditorium at Mountain View Academy. Chatter and giggles from the children filled the space.

Hannah stepped up to the microphone. "Does anyone else have a question for Mr. Beckett?"

Earlier, when Cody and Ellie arrived at the school, Hannah had broken the news that Principal Murray had called an assembly. She thought having the entire student body present would be a great way to educate the children on the importance of service dogs, and their role in assisting people with challenges.

Soft voices echoed through the auditorium, but no one raised their hand. Hannah stepped closer to the microphone. "If you don't have questions, let's give Mr. Beckett and Ellie a big round of applause before you head to your classrooms or to the cafeteria."

The children clapped and filed out of the room in an orderly fashion.

"Thank you again for coming this morning. I think the children enjoyed it." Hannah gathered a few papers off the podium.

"It was my pleasure. My brothers and I love to share the benefits of handling a service animal." Cody looked around at the empty stage. He needed an opportunity to speak with Hannah alone. Volunteering to train a dog took commitment. Cody had his share of people who were excited and willing at first, but failed to follow through. "Do you need to get back to the classroom?"

"No, my class has their lunch period. In fact, if you'd like to join McKenzie and Madison in the cafeteria, I can take Ellie back to my classroom. I'd love to spend some time with her." Hannah reached down and scratched the top of the dog's head.

No time like the present. "I was hoping we'd have a couple of minutes to talk about your offer to help me train Ellie." He held his breath waiting for an answer.

Hannah glanced at her watch and blinked several times.

Cody's instincts were correct. Hannah's body language told the story. She chewed on her lower lip and avoided eye contact.

"Yeah…um, after going over my calendar, I'm not sure it's the best time for me to commit myself." She tucked a strand of hair behind her ear. "You know—with the holidays and all."

It hadn't been his imagination. When he'd mentioned Ellie would be handled by someone with PTSD, it had definitely sparked a negative reaction from Hannah.

An uncomfortable silence hung in the air. Hannah fingered the gold cross around her neck. "I'm sorry. I should have never volunteered so quickly." She glanced at the floor. "It's just… Ellie instantly captured my heart."

Cody knew little about Hannah. Maybe she had family coming to visit for the holidays or perhaps she had plans to leave town while the kids were on winter break. Still, the feeling that there was more to her change of heart clung to him like a polyester T-shirt on a humid summer day. "I totally understand. And I appreciate your honesty."

"Thank you for being so understanding." Hannah smiled. "I'd still like to take Ellie to my classroom if you want to join McKenzie and Madison in the cafeteria."

"I'd like that. Hopefully, the girls won't feel embarrassed by their old uncle," Cody laughed.

"I'm sure they'll be happy to spend time with you. After you're finished eating, you can walk back with them and pick up Ellie." Hannah hoisted her tote bag from behind the podium and flung it over her shoulder.

Cody nodded and exited the auditorium. He thought about extending an offer to Hannah to come and visit Ellie any time, but he held his tongue. It was best if he kept his relationship with Hannah on a professional level. She was the teacher and he was the parent. Besides, Hannah Simpson was the type of woman he could easily fall for. His focus needed to stay on the twins and the upcoming Christmas festival. Tucked inside a binder, he had all the ideas he planned to present to the mayor later this afternoon. But, as he moved down the hallway to the cafeteria, Cody couldn't get Hannah's adorable dimples out of his mind.

"Hello, Miss Simpson. I hope the disposal is working well for you." The gentleman tipped his brown cowboy hat as he hurried along the downtown sidewalk.

"Good afternoon, Mr. Whitfield. Yes, it's working fine. Thank you." Hannah smiled. When she'd first moved into her rental property, Hannah had issues with the garbage disposal. Within one hour of placing the call to her landlord, Nelson Whitfield, the town plumber, had arrived. Dressed in faded overalls and heavy boots, Nelson welcomed Hannah and fixed the problem within fifteen minutes. He'd even extended a dinner invitation to join him and his wife after church one Sunday. His genuine smile had never left his face. Smiles were ubiquitous in Bluebell Canyon.

Hannah took in her surroundings. A sense of calmness filled her body. She longed to bottle this feeling, free from the agony of loss. But was she putting too much expectancy on the town? Believing the townspeople could help put an end to her panic attacks? This was what she prayed for each morning.

Outside of Garrison's Mercantile, her heart squeezed at the festive trimmings covering the front window. Her daughter, Jenna, adored Christmas decorations. After Hannah washed the last plate from their Thanksgiving meal, Jenna begged for her father to bring the boxes of ornaments from the attic. Rick believed it was premature, but when it came to his daughter's love of Christmas, he always gave in.

Hannah quickly looked away and headed inside the store. The overhead bell jingled. She grabbed a basket and moved toward the grocery aisle. Following the deaths of Rick and Jenna, shopping for groceries left Hannah feeling empty. Everything she'd once happily purchased for her family was now a painful reminder. At least shopping for one meant a quick trip in and out.

"Hello, my dear." A welcoming voice pulled Hannah from her thoughts and the possibility of experiencing another panic attack.

Nellie Garrison approached Hannah as she tossed a box of dog treats into the basket. Although she'd withdrawn her offer to volunteer with training, Hannah still hoped she could visit Ellie before the dog would be paired with a handler.

"Hi, Mrs. Garrison." Nellie was the first person she'd met in town. The day she took the keys to her new home, her landlord mentioned Garrison's Mercantile was the place to shop for groceries and sundries. Nellie's demeanor was like Hannah's favorite aunt, who'd passed away two years prior. Hannah had instantly felt a connection to Nellie.

She placed a hand on Hannah's arm. "Please, call me Nellie. Can I help you find something?"

"I just dropped in to pick up a couple of items." She took a quick glance at her watch. With another hour until her meeting with the mayor, Hannah slowed down to enjoy a friendly conversation.

"Are those for Ellie?" Nellie pointed to the treats.

Hannah gave a closed-lip smile. "Uh—how did you know?" Yes, Bluebell Canyon was a small town, but this was beyond belief.

"Since you've volunteered to help Cody train Ellie, I just assumed they'd be for her. As far as I know, you don't have a dog of your own."

Hannah stifled a laugh. Was there actually news that hadn't funneled through Nellie's store? "I suppose you didn't hear. I had to withdraw my offer to help train Ellie. I have so many commitments already with Thanksgiving and Christmas right around the corner."

Nellie folded her hands in front of her polka-dotted apron. "Oh, that's a shame. Cody is such a wonderful young man. The two of you would be perfect for each other. He could definitely use a little motherly influence around the house, especially after he adopts McKenzie and Madison."

Hannah's ears perked up. She thought Cody hadn't decided about adopting, but she kept her thoughts to herself. "I hate to quash your plans for doing a little matchmaking, but I'm not looking to get involved with anyone." *Maybe never.* The pain of losing someone you love made falling in love again undesirable.

"Fiddle-de-dee." Nellie grinned. "Once you spend time with Cody, you'll change your mind. He's a wonderful man."

The telephone rang behind the counter. "Excuse me a minute."

Hannah's shoulders relaxed. Grateful for the interruption, she hurriedly grabbed a few more items. With the freckled-face teenage boy working the register, maybe she could make an escape before Nellie finished her call. Hannah had grown to love the woman, but the last thing she wanted was for Nellie or anyone to play cupid.

Forty-five minutes later, Hannah sat in the reception area of the mayor's office. An oversize bowl of complimentary peppermint candies sat on the coffee table in front of the sofa. Despite the cold temperature outside, a vase of fresh-cut flowers on the front desk provided a sweet reminder of spring.

With a leather-bound journal in her lap, Hannah reviewed her list of suggestions she'd compiled for the Christmas festival. Her earlier reaction to the window display had confirmed her belief. If she could push through the painful memories organizing the event could trigger, it might help her manage the panic attacks. Maybe even stop them for good.

The computer on the front desk chimed. During an earlier exchange of pleasantries, Hannah learned Jennifer, the receptionist, had worked in the mayor's office for the past twenty years.

"The mayor will see you now," Jennifer announced.

Hannah stood. The nearby door creaked opened.

"It's good to see you, Hannah." The mayor waved a hand toward the office. "Please come in." The portly, balding man had a welcoming smile.

"It's nice to see you again too, sir." She stepped inside. Her eyes immediately went to the large mahogany desk situated underneath an arched window providing an amazing view of the Rockies.

"Please, call me Jared." Mayor Jennings moved to the conference table across the room.

Hannah pulled out the leather chair and took a seat. It was then she realized the mayor gave up his view in order to allow his guests to enjoy it. "I see why you have your back to the window."

Jared laughed. "When I was first elected and settled into this office, I learned quickly I wouldn't get any work accomplished facing that view." He reached for the pitcher in the center of the table and filled three glasses with water. "Here you go." He passed the beverage.

"Thank you." Hannah watched as Jared placed one glass in front of his leather portfolio and the other in front of the empty seat next to hers. "Are you expecting someone else?" Perhaps he'd asked Jennifer to join them and take notes.

Voices sounded outside in the reception area.

The mayor stood. "Actually, I am." He moved to the door behind Hannah. "Hello Cody, please come in and join us."

Hannah spun in her chair. She'd heard the mayor correctly. Cody towered in the doorway. He was the last person she expected to see. Judging by the surprised look on his face, the feeling was mutual.

Jared chuckled. "You two look like deer caught in the headlights. Have a seat next to Hannah." He motioned first to Cody and then to the vacant chair.

Hannah picked up her glass of water and gulped down half of its contents.

Cody sat in the chair. He repeated Hannah's action, but he drank the entire glass. He placed the empty glassware on the table. "I'm a little surprised to see Hannah here. Did I confuse the date or time of our meeting?"

The same thought would have crossed Hannah's mind if she wasn't so meticulous in managing her calendar. She ran a finger down the side of her glass and waited for an explanation to clear up the obvious scheduling error. Surely Cody had a mix-up with the date and would leave so she and the mayor could have their meeting.

Mayor Jennings cleared his throat and sat down. "When the town lost the organizer for this year's Christmas festival, a part of me thought I might have to cancel the two-weekend event. Although the town isn't lacking kindhearted people who never hesitate to lend a helping hand, I was afraid no one would volunteer. This position requires a lot of time and dedication, especially now that we're in a time crunch. With that said, I was thrilled when I not only got one, but two volunteers." He passed his gaze over Cody and then to Hannah. "Thank you both. I think you two will work wonderfully together. I have complete faith you'll give Bluebell Canyon their best festival ever."

Hannah turned to Cody. His eyes were fixated in her direction. Was he smiling? Her heart raced, but it wasn't because of his handsome good looks. It was fear. What if she experienced a panic attack in front of him? There was no way she could work closely in the coming weeks to put together a successful Christmas festival with him. But how could she back out now?

Chapter Four

~~

"Uncle Cody, don't forget we're in charge of bringing the pumpkin pies to the Garrisons' house tomorrow for Thanksgiving." McKenzie looked up and dropped her spoon into her cereal bowl. Milk splashed on the table.

"You're making a mess." Madison picked up her napkin and wiped the wooden tabletop.

McKenzie scrunched her face. "I didn't mean to. The spoon slipped out of my hand."

Cody flung the dish towel onto the counter and headed to the grocery list posted on the refrigerator. Before the twins came to live with him, Cody had never kept a grocery list in his life.

Shopping for one was easy. Everything was by memory. Lately, with McKenzie's antics at school, Cody's mind was like a scrambled egg. "I'll pick up some pies later this morning when I go to Garrison's Mercantile for the rest of the items I need."

"We can't take a pie that Mrs. Garrison made." McKenzie rolled her eyes. "We need to bake it."

Cody hadn't given it a second thought, but McKenzie was right. Taking one of Nellie's own pies was odd, but he didn't know the first thing about baking. As a young boy, he'd watch his mother in the kitchen. She made everything look easy. "Do you know how to make a pie?" Cody looked at McKenzie.

McKenzie chewed on her lower lip. "Kind of."

"No, you don't," Madison refuted. "I know how to make cupcakes, but pies aren't as easy. Making the crust is impossible." Madison crinkled her brow.

Cody needed to stick with his first thought. Buy the pie. "We've got a full day today. There's no time for baking. Mrs. Garrison won't mind. It's the gesture that counts." He glanced at the clock on the microwave. "Your uncle Jake and the family will be here at nine o'clock to take you both to Denver for the day, so finish your breakfast."

"I can't wait to see the state Christmas tree when they turn on the lights!" Madison bounced in her seat and looked at Cody. "It would be much better if you could go with us to the outdoor ice rink and to see the tree."

Madison's words warmed Cody's heart while simultaneously increasing his pulse. As much as he wanted to give the girls a memorable Christmas, his feelings were mixed about spending the afternoon alone with Hannah. During their meeting with the mayor, Cody sensed Hannah probably had a few reservations herself. As difficult as it might be, he'd have to keep his focus on the festival and off Hannah's adorable dimples and perky little nose.

"He's working with Miss Simpson today—remember?" McKenzie reminded her twin. "They're planning the Christmas festival."

Cody observed McKenzie nudge her sister and then wink.

Madison stifled a giggle. "Oh, yeah. I guess that's more important."

Something was up with the girls. Cody couldn't quite put a finger on it. Were Madison and McKenzie trying to play matchmaker? How could that be? They were only six years old. At their age, he knew nothing about adult relationships. "I want you girls to have fun with your cousins today. We'll all meet up later for dinner and you can tell me all about it."

"I almost forgot! It's pizza night. Mr. Pepperoni has the best pizza ever!" Madison cheered.

Since moving to Colorado from Virginia, the family had pizza night the evening before Thanksgiving. It was a tradition established by his mother long before her Alzheimer's diagnosis. Although she and their father no longer took part, the brothers maintained the holiday custom.

"Maybe you should invite Miss Simpson, Uncle Cody," McKenzie suggested, while cupping her hands together.

Cody's instincts were correct. The girls wanted him and Hannah to spend as much time as possible together. It was imperative that he keep in mind that his time with their beautiful teacher was to help the mayor out of a jam. But more importantly, he hoped volunteering would give him the confidence he'd need to make the biggest decision of his life.

Later that morning, after Jake and Olivia had picked up the twins for their trip to Denver, Cody headed into town. After picking up what he needed at Garrison's Mercantile, he still had a good thirty minutes to review his notes before the scheduled ten-thirty appointment with Hannah.

Outside the window of the Hummingbird Café, a light snow had fallen early, dusting the quaint streets of Bluebell Canyon. The fireplace in the corner crackled and popped, creating a warm and cozy atmosphere. Cody's stomach squeezed. Maybe he should have suggested meeting at the library. He'd never thought of the café as a romantic spot, but the idea of sitting across from Hannah brainstorming ideas got his heart racing with excitement.

Cody pushed himself away from the table and grabbed his notebook.

"I thought you had a meeting." Sally approached the table as Cody stood, ferrying a pot of steaming coffee.

The last thing Cody wanted to do was admit he needed to

step outside in the thirty-degree air. That his thoughts about meeting Hannah had him feeling like a teenager with his first case of puppy love. "I do. I thought I'd step out on the porch for a little fresh air."

"Oh goodness. Is the fireplace too warm for you? I knew I shouldn't have thrown on that extra log. Mrs. Buser was in earlier and complained about the chill." Sally glanced toward the roaring flames.

"No, the fire is perfect." If you wanted to impress a certain young lady by inviting her to a romantic establishment, it was fine. The truth was, it wasn't the place triggering these ideas. Cody loved this café. It was thoughts of Hannah causing these conflicting emotions.

"Okay, but I'll hold off putting any additional logs on the fire." Sally turned and headed back inside, and Cody stepped through the front doors of the café.

"I'm not late, am I?"

Cody had no sooner pushed the picture out of his mind of him and Hannah snuggling by the fire when he spotted her scurrying up the front steps of the café. Dressed in winter-white corduroy pants and a white down jacket, she looked like an adorable snow bunny. He quickly glanced at his watch. From what Cody knew of Hannah, she struck him as the kind of person who was always punctual. "Actually, you're right on time. I just stepped outside for a breath of fresh air. Sally has the fireplace going."

"If it's too warm for you inside, we can work over there." Hannah pointed to the empty bistro table situated under the bright winter sunlight. The earlier snow was now a distant memory. "It might get us into a more festive mood if we do our planning outdoors."

Cody pounced on her suggestion. If working outside could shake off the romantic thoughts swirling in his head, he was all for it. "That sounds like a great idea. We can even walk around town a little to do some brainstorming."

"That's exactly what I was thinking," Hannah said, nodding. "No one has offered to give me a tour of your town."

"Well then, let me be the first. I'll run inside and give Sally a heads-up that we're changing tables. Would you like a cup of coffee?"

"Actually, I'd love some hot chocolate with extra marshmallows." Her eyes sparkled in the sun.

"You got it. I'll be right back." Cody spun on the heel of his boot and headed inside. He was excited to give Hannah a personal walking tour.

Minutes later, Cody rejoined Hannah at the table. "Sally will be out in a minute with your hot chocolate."

"Sounds great." Hannah opened up her binder and flipped through several pages.

Cody took notice of the brightly colored highlighted pages with matching tabs. Obviously, Hannah wasn't lacking in organizational skills.

Hannah scribbled on a page using a neon pink pen. "I thought with you being a longtime resident of Bluebell Canyon, you could fill me in on the activities offered from past Christmas festivals."

"By the looks of that binder, I think you might have more ideas for the town festival than they've ever had."

Hannah laughed and pushed her hair away from her face. "I guess you can say I'm pretty detail oriented. Once I brainstorm an idea, more ideas keep coming. I'm embarrassed to say I have another notebook almost filled at home. I didn't want to scare you off, so I thought I'd just bring this one with me today."

"With your head so full of ideas, maybe you should think about writing a book." Cody had a bull rider friend who'd left the rodeo circuit to write western novels. The last time they'd spoken, he'd hit the bestseller list.

Hannah's cheeks flushed. "I'm working on one now."

"Really? That's terrific. What kind of book are you writing?" Cody leaned forward with interest.

"It's a romance." Her eyes danced from him back to her notebook and she blushed.

"Don't be embarrassed. From what I hear, romance is the hottest selling genre on the market right now."

"I guess I just feel silly talking about it with a man. Men aren't usually the target audience for a romance novel." Hannah tucked a strand of hair behind her ear.

"So you don't think I've ever read a romance book?"

Hannah's brow arched. "Have you?"

Busted. "Well—no, but yours could be the first." He smiled.

Sally worked her way across the patio ferrying a tray. "Two hot chocolates with extra marshmallows." She placed an oversize mug in front of Hannah. Gooey marshmallow foam clung to the rim of the cup.

"Yum—this looks delicious. Thank you." Hannah licked her lower lip.

"Let me know if you need anything else." Sally placed Cody's drink on the table and smiled.

"Thanks, Sal."

Cody waited for Hannah to take the first sip. He was curious whether she'd have the same reaction he'd had the first time he tasted the creamy concoction. Sally's secret recipe had been passed down through generations. Cody was never able to identify the special ingredient that gave the drink a spicy kick.

"Oh my. This is the best hot chocolate I've ever tasted." Hannah looked up with a dollop of marshmallow foam stuck to the tip of her nose.

Cody laughed and pulled a napkin from the dispenser. "May I?" He leaned forward. "You've got a little on your nose."

Hannah blushed for a second time since joining Cody. She placed her finger along the edge of the mug, gave it a quick swipe and licked her finger.

Despite his best intentions, his gaze was drawn to her lips coated with sticky sweetness. "Do you want me to ask Sally for some more marshmallows?" Cody joked.

Hannah glanced down at her beverage. "When I was a little girl, I would beg my mother for more marshmallows. Once I remember her filling the cup with three big handfuls before pouring the hot chocolate overtop. The marshmallows went over the top and all over the table. We both laughed until we cried."

Cody smiled. "It sounds like you had a great childhood."

"I was blessed with wonderful parents. They're in a retirement home in Florida, but they remain active."

"That's good to hear." A shadow of doubt crossed Cody's mind. Was he capable of providing the same for McKenzie and Madison? Lately, with McKenzie acting out in school, he wasn't so sure. If he allowed himself to think into the future, his doubts seemed to increase. What did he know about teenage girls and the problems they might face? Following Pastor Kidd's advice to take things one day at a time was becoming more difficult as the adoption date grew near.

"Do you mind if I take a look at what other ideas you've come up with?" Cody asked.

Following an hour of small talk and sharing a few childhood memories, it was time to get down to business. The delightful feeling of her heart skipping a beat each time Cody smiled was nice, but as much as she enjoyed Cody's company and hearing stories from his past, she needed to set boundaries in order to keep her focus on her goal. By ensuring the town of Bluebell Canyon had their best Christmas festival ever could perhaps keep her mind occupied and get her through the first Christmas without her family.

Hannah thumbed through several pages, popped open the pink three-ring binder and removed four sheets of paper. Pink had been her daughter's favorite color. Each page contained bulleted suggestions along with detailed descriptions. She passed her ideas across the table.

Cody reviewed the pages and blinked several times while shifting in his seat. "I'm not sure there's anything left for me to add."

Hannah had waited expectantly for a positive reaction, but instead she noticed that Cody's shoulders slumped. His earlier excitement for preparing for the festival seemed to come down a couple of notches.

"Is something wrong?" Hannah bit her lower lip.

Cody shook his head. "No…it's just at first glance, I'm thinking maybe the mayor should have allowed you to take control of the planning. By the looks of this list, there's enough activities to fill not only a two-weekend festival but to carry us into the New Year."

Hannah leaned forward, and a mix of concern and determination stirred within her. "I didn't mean to overwhelm you with ideas. Please know, I'm not trying to take full control. Obviously, being a longtime resident of Bluebell Canyon, you know much more about the town and what the people expect of the festival."

Cody sighed and raked a hand through his hair. "I might know the people, but I've never planned a big event like this. Maybe I bit off more than I can chew by volunteering. I can hardly handle the twins these days."

The past couple of days, McKenzie had created some disruptions in class, but Hannah had held off getting Cody involved. He had a lot on his plate. Besides, Hannah believed McKenzie's actions were merely to attract attention, something that wasn't uncommon given the twins' circumstances. "You're too hard on yourself. I think you're doing a great job with the girls. In fact, they've talked endlessly about how much they enjoy helping you with Ellie and the other dogs."

Cody relaxed his shoulders. "Thanks for sharing that with me. Their moods are so up-and-down. I have a hard time telling what they like and don't like. It seems to change by the hour."

Hannah laughed. "They are just being typical little girls." Her thoughts immediately went to Jenna. Her daughter had been the same at that age, always changing her mind.

Cody hesitated for a moment. "I think they'd be a lot happier if you reconsidered and helped us with Ellie. You seemed excited at first and Ellie obviously connected with you. Are you sure you can't find the time?"

Interesting enough, Hannah had been praying over that very thing. Maybe working with Ellie could help in controlling the panic attacks. And just like she'd hoped with planning the festival, it could help her to keep her mind off of the loss of her family. "Actually, last night I was looking over my calendar and if the offer still stands, I'd love to help."

"Really? That's great. The girls will be so happy." Cody smiled. "You're probably headed out of town for Thanksgiving, but if you're home on Saturday, the twins and I plan to work with Ellie. We'd love for you to join us."

Hannah initially planned to cook a chicken breast, perhaps even a little stuffing. She'd spend Thanksgiving in her small cottage alone, watching classic holiday movies. The movies were a tradition she shared with her family. That had been her plan until she received the unexpected invitation. "I have plans for Thanksgiving, but I'll be in town. Nellie Garrison was kind enough to invite me to their home tomorrow. In fact, once we're finished here, I'll have to head home to do some cooking. I can't go empty handed."

"That's great you'll be attending the Garrisons' annual turkey fry. You'll have the opportunity to meet practically everyone in town. It's always a big shindig and a lot of fun. The twins and I will be there too. The weather should be perfect." Cody paused and tilted his head in her direction. "Any chance I can pay you to bake a pie?"

"Excuse me?" Hannah couldn't ignore Cody's serious expression.

"My plan was to purchase a couple pumpkin pies at Garrison's Mercantile today. But when I mentioned it to the twins this morning, McKenzie was adamant that taking pies Nellie baked was socially unacceptable." Cody placed his elbows on the table, pressed his fingers against his eyelids and sighed.

Hannah laughed. "I kind of see her point." Once upon a time, during the holidays, Hannah loved to turn on Christmas music and bake in her kitchen. Since her move to Bluebell Canyon, she'd yet to break in the new oven installed prior to her moving into the home. "I'd be happy to bake a pie for you to take. And it won't cost you a dime. I love to bake. It's a hobby of mine."

"No, no. I was only joking. I accepted Nellie's invitation and it's my responsibility to show up with something. The girls know how to make the pie, it's just the crust they find challenging. I thought maybe we could make pumpkin pudding instead."

"You're more than welcome to come to my house. I can show you how to make the crust. It's not that difficult." Hannah extended the offer with little thought.

"Really? That would be great. It could save me the embarrassment of presenting Nellie with one of her own pies at her door. If I'm a quick study, I could even teach the girls what I learned. Maybe then at Christmas we can bake our own."

It was then Hannah realized Cody didn't intend to include the girls today. Her chest tightened. "So you won't be bringing McKenzie and Madison with you?"

"No, the girls went up to Denver today with my brother and

his family for the Christmas tree lighting. They have tons of activities going on, so they're spending the day."

Planning the Christmas festival in a public place with Cody was one thing, but spending the afternoon alone together baking in her kitchen didn't sound like a good idea. In fact, it was a terrible idea. She certainly didn't want to send him the wrong message. "Since I already planned to bake, I can make the pie for you."

"I couldn't ask that of you. Besides, this could be an opportunity for me to impress the girls. My cooking skills aren't exactly gourmet. We eat a lot of macaroni and cheese. That's my specialty. Not the box kind either. I make it homemade." Cody straightened his shoulders.

Hannah laughed. "It's only a pie."

"To you it is. But for me, it's an opportunity to expand my dinner menu beyond mac and cheese. If I learn to bake a pie, I could make homemade potpies. The girls love chicken."

Hannah's heart stilled and her chest relaxed. How could she take back her offer? Cody only wanted to provide for the girls. It seemed like yesterday that she'd struggled with what to cook her family for dinner. And she was skilled in the kitchen. It couldn't be easy for Cody. Hannah checked her watch and closed the binder before losing her nerve. "Let's wrap this up for now."

"Does that mean you're giving me the green light to come over for my first official baking lesson?" Cody glanced at her and his eyes twinkled.

Hannah gulped at the response she had to Cody's glance. Was she wrong to let down her guard? Too late now. Remembering the freshly laundered clothing she'd dumped on the sofa and the plan to fold upon her return home, she'd need a head start. "Why don't we meet at my place at two o'clock? Since I have a double oven, we can do some additional planning for the festival while the pies are baking."

"That sounds perfect. It will give me time to run to Garrison's Mercantile for the ingredients, along with a few other items. Do you want me to pick up anything for you?" Cody offered.

"No, thank you. I have everything I need to make a sweet potato casserole."

"Great. Maybe you can teach me how to make that, too. The twins love sweet potatoes." Cody started to push away from the table but stopped. "I planned on buying us lunch today. How about I pick up some sandwiches and bring them over?"

Hannah only had coffee for her breakfast, and the mention of food caused a response deep in her belly. "I am a little hungry. A turkey and Swiss on rye would be wonderful." Hannah reached for her purse and removed her wallet.

Cody put up a hand. "No, lunch is on me."

Hannah nodded. "At least let me pick up the tab for all of the hot chocolate I drank."

"You can buy next time." Cody stood and grabbed his jacket off the back of the chair.

"Wait—don't you need my address?" Hannah ripped a piece of paper from her notepad.

Cody reached for Hannah's hand. "This is Bluebell Canyon. Everyone knows where you live. See you at two o'clock." He flashed a smile, spun on his heel and headed to the register to settle their bill.

A twinge of excitement ignited in her body. Hannah couldn't deny she liked the idea of spending more of the afternoon with Cody. Normally, her weekends were spent alone doing housework and preparing her classroom lessons for the upcoming week. It would be nice to have some company in the kitchen, but she'd have to remember their time together was for the town and the twins—nothing more.

Chapter Five

At five minutes before two, Cody pulled his truck into the short driveway lined with boxwood shrubs. He'd shopped for the groceries at record speed, anxious to spend more time with Hannah.

The charming two-bedroom cottage was nestled in a quiet neighborhood of seven additional homes. In the years Cody had lived in Bluebell Canyon, the home was owned by George and Mona Lawson. After their passing, the eldest son, who lived in Texas, had kept the property as a rental.

Cody always loved the home, with its quaint front porch adorned with weathered wooden railings. The gently sloped roof with aged cedar shakes gave the house character, as did the large picture windows framed in knotty pine lining the front of the home.

Hannah had made an excellent choice to move her life to Bluebell Canyon. Of course, Cody didn't know about Hannah's plans. The truth was, he really didn't know much about Hannah. So far, she'd kept her past quiet. The same could be said about him and his broken relationship with Mallory. Perhaps today they could learn a little more about each other. If all went well, he even planned to take McKenzie's suggestion and invite her to pizza night tonight with his family.

Cody unfastened his seat belt and stepped out of the vehicle.

"Do you need some help?" Hannah poked her head outside of the front door.

Had she been anxious for his arrival? He shook off the thought. Maybe she was just ready to get it over with. During the drive from the market to Hannah's house, Cody questioned whether he'd been too forward by crashing the quiet afternoon of baking she'd initially planned. It was too late now. "Sure, I could use a hand." He waved and smiled.

Hannah smiled, pulled the door closed and scurried down the steps.

"I'll grab the groceries. You take the sandwiches." Cody passed the bag containing the freshly made deli subs. "With Nellie's freshly baked bread combined with Hank's sandwich-making skills, you're in for a treat."

"I can't wait. I'm starving." Hannah took the food and they headed inside.

The house was as cozy as Cody remembered. "I always loved this place," Cody remarked, following Hannah across the hardwood floor covering the small foyer and into the open kitchen with cheery yellow walls.

"You've been inside?" Hannah placed the bag on the granite countertop and pulled two plates from the pine cabinet.

Cody unpacked the sandwiches and two bags of chips. "Many times. George, the original owner, always liked to do projects around the house. My brothers and I would often lend a hand."

"That's nice. I've always wanted to live in a small town where neighbors help one another." Hannah placed the sandwich labeled *roast beef* on a plate and passed it to Cody. Then she put the turkey sub on the other dish.

"Well, you've come to the right place. The people in Bluebell Canyon look out for one another. You won't find a tighter-knit community."

Hannah removed two glasses from the cabinet and filled them with ice. "Is sweet tea okay with you?"

"That sounds perfect." Cody carried the sandwiches and chips to the farmhouse-style table, situated to take advantage of the mountain view through the large bay window.

Hannah removed the pitcher of sweet tea from the refrigerator and joined Cody. "Is there anything else you need?"

"Looks good to me. Let's eat." Cody followed Hannah's lead and took a seat at the table.

Hannah unwrapped her sandwich and took a large bite. "Yum…this is the best turkey sandwich I've ever had."

Cody laughed. He liked to see a woman with a healthy appetite. "I told you. You won't find one better anywhere in Colorado." He took a drink of his sweet tea. "So, I don't know much about you. Where are you originally from?"

Hannah's shoulders stiffened in response to his question. It was obvious she didn't like to talk about herself, but he wanted to learn more about her. At the same time, he didn't want to make her uncomfortable. "I'm sorry. If you'd rather we talk about something else, that's fine."

Hannah picked up her napkin and blotted her lips. "No, it's all right. I'm from Phoenix, Arizona. It's the only home I've ever known—until now."

Cody nodded and refrained from asking another question. It was best to let Hannah volunteer any details about her past life in Phoenix. According to her, she'd had a good childhood, but maybe that wasn't the case in her adult years. They'd be spending a lot of time together between the festival planning and training Ellie. Maybe in time, she'd offer more about herself. There was no reason to push her even though he was dying to know everything about her.

Following lunch and a quick cleanup, Hannah passed an apron to Cody. "You might want to wear this. You can tie it around your waist."

"Are you sure this is necessary?" Cody had never worn an apron in his life. Much less one covered with red hearts along with *Kiss the Cook* printed in bold, red lettering across the front.

Hannah secured another apron around her waist and laughed. "Relax, I won't take any photos. You'll thank me once we begin to work with the flour. It can make a mess of your clothes, particularly your dark denim." She gestured toward the ingredients she'd neatly arranged on the counter. "We'll each make our own crust. You follow my lead. The recipe for my crust calls for all-purpose flour, salt, cold unsalted butter and ice water."

Cody scratched underneath his chin. "Wouldn't it be easier to buy an already made crust?"

"Taking the narrow path isn't always the best." She paused and pushed a strand of hair away from her face with the backside of her hand. "At least, that's what I've learned. Besides, it will taste much better when you create it from scratch."

"I'm not so sure." Cody raised an eyebrow.

"Relax, you'll do fine." Hannah glanced at Cody while continuing to proceed with a practiced hand. "We'll whisk together the salt and flour in this mixing bowl."

"Got it. What's next?" Cody observed then copied her movements.

Hannah's hand brushed Cody's as she reached for a small stick of cold unsalted butter. "We'll add this butter into the flour mixture. It's important that the butter is cold."

He tried to ignore the warm sensation traveling up his arm following her touch. "Why is that?"

Using a pastry cutter, she blended the butter into the flour, creating a coarse crumb-like mixture in each mixing bowl. "Cold butter will help to create a flaky crust."

Hannah moved on to the next step. "Now, we add the ice

water." She sprinkled two tablespoons of ice water over the mixture and gently stirred.

"Only two?" Cody looked at her sideways.

"No, you can continue to add the water, one tablespoon at a time, until the dough comes together."

Cody followed the instructions and gave Hannah a slight nudge. "This isn't as hard as I thought it would be." He winked. "Or maybe it's because you make it seem so easy."

"Be careful not to overwork it, though. It should still look kind of crumbly, but we want it to hold together when pinched." Hannah turned and cleaned the adjacent counter. Next she sprinkled a fistful of flour over the surface before returning to her dough.

Cody carefully followed Hannah's instructions and gradually incorporated the water. "Yeah, I see what you mean," he remarked as the dough slowly took shape. "This could be a good lesson for the girls on the importance of taking your time and being patient." Perhaps it could be a good lesson for him as well.

"You're right. Children don't always have patience," Hannah said with a gentle smile. "Now it's time to form the dough." She transferred the mixture onto the clean and floured counter. "Gently gather the dough into a ball and flatten it into a disk." She watched as Cody mirrored her actions. "If the dough appears dry, you can add a little more water, but be careful not to put in too much."

Cody added the tiniest bit of water to moisten the dough.

"Perfect." Hannah reached for the box of plastic wrap. "Now, we'll wrap the dough and place it in the refrigerator to chill," Hannah explained.

"What will that do?"

"Chilling the dough for at least thirty minutes allows the gluten to relax and the butter to solidify."

Cody wrapped his disk of dough. "And that's a good thing?"

"It will make it easier to roll out. Dough can be tough to work with sometimes."

Cody nodded. "I'll have to let Olivia in on that tip. The last time she made homemade pizza, she fought with the dough. She'd roll it out and it would roll back in."

Hannah laughed. "Dough can be temperamental." She turned on the faucet and rinsed her hands, then placed the dough into the refrigerator. "Now we wait. Let's have a seat at the table."

"Good idea." Cody washed his hands and removed his apron, happy to sit down and hopefully learn a little more about Hannah.

Hannah took a seat and slid her binder in front of her. "I thought we could do some more festival planning." She passed him another bulleted list of items.

Cody shook off the disappointment. Hannah was right. They needed to keep their focus on the festival. As hard as it might be to keep his eyes off of Hannah, they needed to move forward with their planning. "You have some great ideas. I like the hot chocolate kiosk and offering different flavors of marshmallows and whipped cream."

"Chocolate whipped cream has always been my favorite. What do you think of my other suggestions?" Hannah asked.

"I'm afraid a few might be out of our budget."

Hannah leaned in. "Such as?"

Cody took notice of Hannah's shoulder roll as she sat up a little straighter. "Constructing an outdoor ice rink would not only be costly, but I'm not sure we have enough time for a project such as that."

Hannah tapped her pen against the table. "Maybe not. But, I've been crunching numbers, and the mayor gave me a few names of townspeople who have volunteered their time for any projects we might have. This is exactly what I love about small towns. People stepping up to the plate to support their community."

Cody's stomach twisted.

"I've spoken with several of the business owners in town. They're willing to help with advertising and to contribute financially to the festival fund. They realize the importance of getting the word out. It will only increase foot traffic into their businesses, which will create more revenue."

Cody narrowed his eyes as he leaned back in the chair, crossing his arms over his chest. Not only had Hannah met with the business owners in Bluebell Canyon, but she'd been discussing the festival with the mayor. Why hadn't she mentioned a meeting to him? They could have approached the mayor together. "I thought we were supposed to work as a team?"

"I'm sorry. I didn't mean to overstep my bounds. Yesterday, I ran into the mayor and we chatted. It wasn't a scheduled meeting. I wouldn't do that to you. We're working as a team—I get that. I thought maybe I was doing you a favor—doing us a favor," she added. "You already have a lot on your plate with the twins and your business."

Cody's jaw tightened. "I can handle the girls and my business." Maybe the mayor had been wrong in believing Cody was qualified to organize the festival. And perhaps his friend Scott made the wrong decision when asking Cody to be the guardian to McKenzie and Madison.

The timer on the oven dinged, breaking the silence that hung in the air like a thick fog, but did not ease the tension. The earlier joy Cody felt baking alongside of Hannah had faded.

Hannah pushed away from the table. "I guess we better finish up the pies."

Cody stood and slid his chair underneath the table. He glanced at his watch. "Yeah, I need to get home and take Hershey for a walk before dinner." Cody moved toward the counter while Hannah removed the crusts from the oven. He wouldn't invite Hannah to join his family for pizza night. What would be the point? Her actions made it clear. Hannah didn't need his help with the festival. His stomach churned. Maybe McKenzie and Madison didn't need him either.

The next day, Hannah arrived at the Garrisons' home filled with mixed emotions and a heavy heart. She'd spent the morning reminiscing about past Thanksgiving celebrations with her family. Several times she'd even picked up the phone to call Nellie to say thank you for the invitation, but she was under the weather. Then she received that nudge from God reminding her why she'd come to Bluebell Canyon. It was not to wallow in self-pity. He had given her the opportunity for a fresh start by providing her with an excellent teaching position in a town that was exactly where she needed to be.

Hannah parked her vehicle in the field alongside rows of other cars and exited. The warmth of the sun, along with a slight breeze, provided above-normal temperatures for late November. With a sizable crowd spread about the property, the Thanksgiving gathering appeared to be in full swing.

The aroma of frying turkey filled the air along with mingled sounds of laughter and cheerful conversations. Rows of picnic tables, each covered with festive tablecloths, lined the large patio off the back of the Garrisons' house.

Hannah marveled at the picturesque scene, but the events of the previous day clouded her thoughts. Speaking to the business owners in Bluebell Canyon and the mayor on her own weighed heavily on her mind. The tension that simmered between them yesterday was obvious. Cody's unease was palpable, but he was right. Maybe she had overstepped her bounds by not including him. The mayor had instructed them to work as a team.

Hannah made her way to the patio. Several of her students greeted her with smiles and waves. She spotted Cody across the yard and expelled a breath. He stood with McKenzie and Madison by his side. Their faces flushed with excitement.

McKenzie turned and pointed. "Miss Simpson's here!"

The twins ran across the grass, but Hershey was faster. The dog raced at lightning speed and reached Hannah.

"Hey, girl." Hannah patted Hershey's head while her tail whished back and forth in the grass. Hershey devoured the attention and smothered Hannah's hand with wet kisses.

"Happy Thanksgiving, Miss Simpson!" the twins sing-songed and danced a little jig.

"Thank you. Happy Thanksgiving to you, too," Hannah answered, and her heart skipped when she saw Cody approaching. Their eyes met. Heat grew underneath her down jacket. She gave the zipper a yank.

"You probably won't need to wear your coat, especially when we start to play games," Madison commented.

"Yeah, Uncle Cody set up the cornhole for Uncle Jake. You can be on my team. I'm pretty good." McKenzie peered up at Hannah.

"I'm not familiar with that game, but you can teach me."

Madison stepped closer. "It's not hard. It's a big wooden board with holes. You just throw a beanbag and try to get it into the hole."

"It's a lot harder than it looks, isn't it, Uncle Cody?" McKenzie addressed Cody as he joined the group. "But he can show you how to play." She tugged on the sleeve of his pullover sweater. Her eyes gleamed with mischief.

It was obvious to Hannah the twins were attempting to play matchmaker.

Cody wanted no part of it. Their eyes met and he offered a polite nod along with a forced smile. The distance between them now felt like an insurmountable chasm. Clearly, he'd rather stay far away from Hannah today, but the twins had other plans.

Hannah desperately wanted to right her wrong. She greeted Cody with a warm smile. "Hey, Cody." Her voice was tinged with a hint of uncertainty. "Happy Thanksgiving."

Hannah's greeting hung in the air for a moment, suspended in the tension around an invisible wall between them.

Finally, Cody's eyes held hers longer than a glance. For a moment, Hannah thought she saw a flicker of something— perhaps regret for the way he'd responded to her good news yesterday? But it vanished as quickly as it had appeared, replaced by a guarded smile. "Happy Thanksgiving. I'm glad you made it out today. You'll have a good time."

The twins' excited chatter about the upcoming cornhole game eased the tension, but Cody remained preoccupied. His gaze shifted toward the house for a moment before turning back to the girls.

"Why don't you run along and join the other children where the games are set up. We'll be down in a few minutes. Take Hershey with you."

"Okay, Uncle Cody. But don't forget, Miss Simpson is on my team for cornhole," McKenzie called out as the girls and Hershey took off to rejoin the festivities.

Determined to mend the rift she'd created, Hannah stepped closer to Cody. "I want to apologize for how things went yesterday. It was wrong of me not to have included you in the meeting with the business owners and my discussion with the mayor. We're partners in this and I totally overstepped my bounds." Hannah cupped her hands together.

Cody's eyes looked over her shoulder, avoiding any contact, but he nodded in acknowledgment. "I appreciate the apology. It's just that, well, it's important that I make this festival the best ever, not only for the town, but especially for McKenzie and Madison. I felt a little blindsided when I learned you didn't include me in your discussions with the business owners and the mayor."

Hannah nodded, understanding his perspective. She probably would have reacted the same, given her controlling nature. "I can see why you felt that way. Going forward, I promise we'll work as a team. No more meetings without both of us present." Hannah took her finger and crossed her heart.

Cody laughed. "McKenzie did the cross-my-heart thing this morning when she promised to clean her room tomorrow. I appreciate your understanding. Maybe we can resume our preparation tomorrow evening?"

Her stomach clenched. Was Cody asking her on a date? Why couldn't they meet during the day? After all, the day after Thanksgiving was a school holiday.

"Don't worry. It's not a date or anything." He offered a smile that made her insides feel fluttery.

Hannah's face warmed. Was her reaction that obvious?

"I was thinking me and the girls could take you on a nighttime walking tour of the town. It might help us to brainstorm more ideas for the Christmas lights and evening activities we could offer at the festival."

Hannah's shoulders relaxed. "That sounds like a wonderful idea. A town or a city always looks so different at night."

"I can't take credit for the idea. McKenzie actually suggested it last night while I was tucking the girls into bed. She also thought we should bring the dogs."

"I'm sure Hershey would love it."

Cody nodded. "And Ellie, too. McKenzie specifically said we need to bring her along since she's your favorite. I'm not sure if you've picked up on it, but it appears the girls are trying to think up ways to get us together." Cody's eyes sparkled as he spoke.

"Yes, I have noticed it." Hannah felt her face warm. The twins' intentions had become obvious to her. She needed to change the subject. "McKenzie is quite intuitive. I do have a soft spot for Ellie, so count me in. It sounds like fun." Hannah couldn't deny the fact that there was something about Ellie. She took an easy breath, embracing her original decision to assist Cody in training Ellie. It would be worth it. Remaining as active as possible within the community could only help to put the past behind her. The only question was…how long would it take?

Chapter Six

Friday evening, Cody drained the last of his hot chocolate and wiped his mouth with the cloth napkin. "Let's finish up so we can give Miss Simpson the walking tour of our town."

"It's going to be so fun!" McKenzie cheered while Madison bounced in her seat.

Hannah snatched another chocolate chip cookie from the plate. "After that delicious Thanksgiving meal yesterday, I didn't think I'd be hungry again for a week, but these cookies are scrumptious. I can't stop eating them."

Earlier, they'd all met at the Hummingbird Café for a quick dinner and dessert. Hershey and Ellie were curled up in a gated off corner by the fireplace on fluffy, oversize pillows. Since Sally was a dog lover, she allowed them in the establishment as long as they stayed away from the dining tables.

"I can get a box to go, if you'd like." Cody winked and struggled to pull his eyes off of Hannah. When she displayed her playful, childlike side, he had to continue to remind himself that their time together was for the benefit of the twins and the town.

"I'd better pass. I have to pace myself during the holiday season or I'll have to buy a new wardrobe after the New Year." Hannah popped the last bite of cookie into her mouth and smiled.

Cody admitted to himself he'd taken a little extra time getting ready. He even opened a bottle of aftershave he'd had in his medicine cabinet for at least a year. On the way to the café, the twins had giggled and whispered in the back seat of his truck about his aftershave. He'd only heard bits and pieces of what they were saying, but he did hear McKenzie say something about how their plan was working. "Okay, then. Girls, put your coats on and we'll head out. I'll go take care of the bill and grab the dogs."

Outside, a few fat snowflakes splattered to the ground. The temperature was cold, but the wind remained calm. Cody inhaled a breath. There was nothing better. "The weather is perfect for our outing. Shall we?"

"Can we walk the dogs?" McKenzie asked.

"Good idea." Cody handed off the leashes to the twins.

Hannah looked around while they moved down the sidewalk. "I'm picturing endless strands of Christmas lights. Fresh pine wreaths on every lamppost with twists of garland going down each pole. Lights throughout the landscape. Huge potted poinsettias lining the entrances to each storefront." Holding a tablet in one hand, Hannah crossed her arms in front of her chest and looked from one end of the sidewalk to the other. "It will be beautiful during the daylight hours. Most importantly, after dark with thousands of twinkling lights decorating the businesses, trees and bushes, it will be magical." Hannah's face shined as she envisioned the scene. "We could even install a sound system throughout the town and play Christmas carols."

"I love Christmas music!" Madison added.

Cody saw dollar signs—lots of them. Hannah's ideas were great, but not within the town's budget.

"And a gigantic Christmas tree with zillions of lights!" McKenzie suggested while jumping up and down. Hershey and Ellie barked in agreement.

"Yeah, and maybe we can have Santa Claus light it up on

Christmas Eve. He could pass out presents to some of the kids in town whose parents can't buy them stuff," Madison added. "Mary Matthews, in our class, said she won't get any Christmas presents this year. Her mom is sick and her dad got hurt at his job."

Cody liked the idea of giving gifts to children of lesser means. He looked back at Madison and smiled. She had a generous heart. Her father would be so proud.

Hannah turned her attention to Cody. "I didn't know this about Mary. Do you know the family well?"

Cody nodded. Eventually Hannah would learn that everyone knows everybody in Bluebell Canyon. "Joe and Joyce are wonderful people. They've had a rough year. On top of Joyce's illness, Joe got hurt while working on a construction project."

"Mary said he fell and messed up his knee. He can't work," McKenzie added.

"We could set up the tree in the town square and have Santa pass out presents. But we'll have to keep an eye on how we allocate the money. Not only for gifts, but overall. The town's budget is limited." Cody addressed Hannah. "Don't get me wrong, I love the idea of going all out, but like I've mentioned before, I don't think we're in a position to organize on such a grand scale."

"We have to dream big. Besides, once you and I pay each business owner a personal visit and get the exact dollar amount they're willing to commit, we can reevaluate some of the more costly activities. One thing we could do that wouldn't be expensive is to host a holiday craft fair for a day or two," Hannah suggested.

"What's that?" Madison asked.

"It's a fair where local artists and bakers can sell homemade crafts or food. It will support the community and add a charming touch to the festival. In addition, it can help drive out-of-town visitors into the local establishments."

McKenzie looked up at Cody. "Isn't that a good idea?"

Hannah smiled and continued. "For example, those delicious cookies at the Hummingbird Café. If visitors enjoy them at the fair, they might want to visit the café to purchase more or try something else."

Hannah's dedication to the festival's success was impressive. Cody admired her determination. "Yes, I think that's a great idea. And you're right, it won't cost us anything. We could even charge the vendor a small rental fee for each table or booth they set up. There are several women in town who would love to sell some of their canned goods, handmade quilts, things like that." Maybe he and Hannah made a good team when they put their heads together. "We can have Nellie put out the word to everyone. She's better than an email blast." Cody laughed.

"Another activity that wouldn't cost any money would be a snowman-making contest." Hannah glanced at the twins. "The children would love it."

"But what if it doesn't snow before the festival?" McKenzie questioned.

"Well, I guess we'd have to rent or have someone donate a snowmaking machine," Hannah said.

Cody couldn't remember a Christmas festival in Bluebell Canyon without snow on the ground. "Or we could take our chances. If there's snow, we'll have the contest. That's a good idea, Hannah."

"Maybe we can have a booth with different flavors of shaved ice." Madison licked her lips. "Cherry is my favorite!"

Hannah smiled. "Mine too. Great idea, Madison. We'll add it to the list." Hannah made a note on her tablet.

"I was thinking early this morning about offering horse-drawn carriage rides. It would be a good way for guests to see the town's decorations, particularly those who might not be familiar with Bluebell Canyon." Cody had texted his brother Jake, since he had a carriage he'd purchased as a surprise for

Olivia on their wedding day. "My brother owns a carriage, so it won't cost anything."

"That's a fantastic idea. Can you imagine how romantic it would be for couples, especially if it were snowing?" Hannah exhibited a dreamy gaze.

Cody noticed Hannah's smile slowly fade as if his suggestion created a longing. Was she the type who'd enjoy a moonlit carriage ride? Silly question. What woman wouldn't love that? Who was he kidding? The thought of such a ride with Hannah filled him with excitement.

"Do you usually get a lot of out-of-town visitors during the festival?" Hannah moved away from the topic of carriage rides.

"Yes, we do. In years past, most neighboring towns typically hosted their large festivals in the fall rather than around Christmas. That's helped to boost our attendance."

Hannah nodded. "Perhaps we could reach out to businesses in those towns to assist us in our advertising. We could offer to do the same for their future festivals."

"You're full of great ideas tonight." Cody smiled, giving Hannah a playful nudge.

"It must be this cold night air." Hannah slowed her pace and tightened the angora scarf hanging around her neck.

"If it's too cold for you, we could call it a night," Cody offered.

"No way. I'm enjoying myself too much." Hannah's eyelashes fluttered.

Cody's pulse ticked up a beat. A part of him didn't want this night to end.

The foursome continued their stroll toward the town square. Cody and Hannah discussed various aspects of the festival while McKenzie and Madison walked ahead with Hershey and Ellie. The dogs sniffed every inch of the sidewalk.

They moved past the enormous fountain, now shut off for the winter. During the warmer months, it was a peaceful spot where people tossed coins or simply sat on a nearby bench to enjoy the soothing sound of flowing water.

"Here it is. This is the heart of our community's gatherings and celebrations." Cody stopped beside the tall flagpole located at the right-hand corner of the square where the twins stood with the dogs. Ellie's and Hershey's tails wagged with excitement. "What do you think?"

Hannah's eyes lit up. She walked closer to the flagpole, rested her hand on the pole and looked around. "It's a perfect space, Cody. I can already picture the Christmas tree towering in the center with people gathered around singing carols."

"Caroling is good. It doesn't cost anything." Cody laughed.

"The pavilion is incredible. The arched roof is amazing," said Hannah, pointing.

"That's mahogany wood." Cody was one of many men in town who volunteered to keep the wood meticulously maintained.

Hannah nodded. "I see that. The intricately carved, ornate patterns on each arch are breathtaking. I've never seen anything like it."

"Those four columns are made of marble quarried from nearby mountains," Cody added.

"It's stunning. We could have some of the local musicians perform. Maybe even have a dance the last night of the festival."

"For kids too?" Madison asked.

The twins danced around the flagpole. The dogs circled alongside them. "We love to dance!" McKenzie called out.

"For the entire town," Hannah answered.

"Can we help decorate the tree when it's here?" Madison asked, her eyes sparkling with excitement.

Cody laughed and tugged on the white, fluffy pom-pom sewn on the top of her hat. "Of course, you can. You and McKenzie can be Santa's little helpers."

"Maybe we can even dress up like elves?" McKenzie chimed

in before she and her sister took off toward the pavilion in the center of the square. Hershey and Ellie followed, nipping at the girls' heels as they climbed the steps.

Cody's heart warmed seeing the twins excited to help with the festival. This was exactly what he hoped for. After losing their father and being uprooted to a new place, he wanted this town to feel like home to them. He longed to provide them with a loving environment and a sense of security. But was he capable of giving them everything they needed?

Hannah turned to Cody and smiled. "I think it's wonderful that the girls are so eager to be a part of this," she said. "It shows how much their community means to them."

Cody nodded in agreement. "That's exactly what I was thinking. They're a big reason why I want to make this festival the best ever, but I don't want to promise more than we can deliver. We have to be realistic. I know you said the business owners are willing to make a financial contribution, but some of them are struggling themselves. I wouldn't want them to feel pressured."

"I understand." Hannah shrugged. "We'll just have to be creative. Try not to worry. I have a feeling that this year the town will have a memorable Christmas festival."

Hannah's enthusiasm was contagious. Some of his initial worries about their conflicting ideas seemed to melt away as they found common ground brainstorming ideas. Cody felt a renewed energy. Maybe he *could* give the twins their best Christmas ever.

Early the following day, Hannah was dressed and ready for a busy day ahead. At four in the morning, her eyes had flown open. She hadn't had a dream like this since before she'd married Rick. A week before Rick had proposed marriage, Hannah had a dream they were already married and raising a family together. Last night's dream wasn't much different, except the man was Cody. McKenzie and Madison were present, but Hannah was pregnant with Cody's child. Hannah was obviously spending too much time with Cody and the girls. But as wrong as the dream felt, her heart was telling her otherwise.

Today, time together wasn't something that could be avoided. Hannah was scheduled to meet Cody at the town square. They planned to work with Ellie. Cody wanted to take the dog out around town. Ellie apparently lacked social skills when it came to ignoring distractions in public places.

While getting ready, Hannah paid more attention than usual to what she wore. She had to mentally prepare herself for the day. She and Cody would be alone since McKenzie and Madison were spending the day with Logan's family. Time spent with Cody meant she'd have to ignore his handsome good looks. The way his eyes crinkled when he smiled. But the one thing she found most attractive about him was impossible for her to ignore. Cody was wonderful with McKenzie and Madison. The love he had for the girls was obvious. She prayed for him to find peace and follow through with plans to adopt the twins. As much as Cody doubted his abilities, they were meant to be a family. He would be a wonderful father.

Hannah grabbed her insulated cup and filled it to the brim with hot coffee. She slipped on her coat, secured the angora scarf around her neck and headed out the front door.

"Hello, Hannah."

"Good morning, Mr. O'Brien." Hannah turned and waved at her elderly neighbor. She didn't know a lot about the man except that he was a widow and he always greeted her with a welcoming smile. He seemed to enjoy tinkering around the yard.

Hannah smiled at the life-size, inflatable reindeer he'd placed in his front yard. In years past, she'd tried to use inflatables as decorations, but they always ended up deflated in the front yard like a pancake. She found it to be a little sad, so she donated the decorations.

Mr. O'Brien continued to busy himself stringing lights around the railing that circled his wraparound porch.

"The decorations look nice," Hannah called out across the property.

Mr. O'Brien pulled his attention away from the task at hand and turned to Hannah. "If you'd like, I can decorate your house for you. My wife was a schoolteacher, so I know what kind of busy schedule you carry."

Her neighbor was the reason Hannah wanted to move to a small town. "That's sweet of you, but I don't have any outdoor decorations." The truth of the matter was, Hannah didn't have any Christmas decorations—indoor or outdoor. After losing her family only days before Christmas, she'd thrown out any reminder of the holiday that had once been her family's favorite time of the year. So why had she volunteered to plan the festival? It was something she asked herself every day since committing to the mayor. It made no sense at first, yet deep within her heart Hannah hoped if she could do this for the town, it would be a giant step toward healing the pain of her past.

"I have plenty to decorate both of our houses. Blanche, my wife, loved Christmas. Before she passed away, every year, on the first day of November, she'd have me climb up into the attic and pull down all of the decorations. Do you know she had three Christmas trees?" He laughed. "I didn't mind. From the moment she began to decorate until the last light was strung up, her smile was brighter than a million lights. That's what I first noticed about her—her smile."

Maybe putting up a few decorations in her own home and not just around the town could be a way for Hannah to conquer the anxiety she felt as Christmas neared. "Blanche must have been a special lady."

"That she was," he said, nodding. "So, what do you say? Let's give your home a little holiday cheer. It can be my gift to you."

How could she say no to such a sweet offer? Hannah glanced over her shoulder. The front of her home looked stark in comparison to Mr. O'Brien's residence. "I think you're right about my house in need of a little cheer. Let's do it…but under one condition."

"Okay, what did you have in mind?" Mr. O'Brien squinted into the morning sun.

"Once you're finished, we'll have a ceremonial lighting. Afterwards, you'll be my guest for dinner. I've been told I make a pretty mean pot of chili."

Mr. O'Brien nodded. "You've got yourself a date, young lady."

Hannah glanced at her watch. She didn't want to be late meeting Cody, but she had planned to drop by the Garrisons' store. She wanted to speak with Nellie about Mary's family. "I need to get going, but promise me one more thing."

"Sure."

"You won't get up on the ladder unless I'm here to hold it for you." Last year, a teacher Hannah worked with in Phoenix had a terrible fall. He was cleaning out the gutters around his house and fell off the ladder. Fortunately, he didn't suffer a head injury, but he did break his collarbone.

"Cross my heart. You enjoy your day." Mr. O'Brien turned and continued to string the lights around the railing, whistling "(There's No Place Like) Home for the Holidays."

Hannah's heart warmed at the memory. Her mother played that song every year on the stereo in the living room. "You do the same. And be careful." Hannah pushed the button on her key fob and climbed into her SUV to head into town.

Inside, she pulled the visor down to obstruct the morning sun peeking through the overcast sky. With light snow in the forecast for later this morning, she hoped the roadways would remain clear until she returned home.

A short drive later, Hannah inhaled the aroma of cinnamon as she stepped inside Garrison's Mercantile. The bell over the door jingled.

Hannah looked around. It appeared she was the only customer in the store. She had hoped that would be the case so she could have a little time to speak with Nellie about Mary's family. After Madison had mentioned Mary yesterday, Hannah couldn't get her student out of her mind. The little girl was always well dressed and seemed to be a happy child. Hannah had no idea what she'd been dealing with at home. Knowing her family struggled with their finances troubled Hannah.

"Good morning, Hannah. Aren't you the early bird this morning?" Nellie buzzed in from the back room, tightening her apron.

"Morning. I have a busy day today, so I thought I'd get an early start. Plus, there was something I wanted to speak with you about. If you have the time." Hannah inhaled a deep breath. "Judging from the delectable aroma coming from your kitchen, I think my timing might be perfect for a change."

"You're right. The first customer of the day always gets a free cinnamon roll. I consider them my guinea pig." Nellie laughed.

"You shouldn't have told me that. I might start camping out on your doorstep," Hannah joked, but she really wasn't. Cinnamon rolls had always been a temptation she couldn't resist.

"Actually, I like having a little company in the early morning hours. Let me get you a roll and some coffee. Take a seat at the counter and I'll be right out." Nellie scurried to the kitchen, obviously excited to have an early visitor.

Hannah took off her coat and scarf and hung them over an empty stool. She settled onto the neighboring seat. Scanning the store, she zeroed in on the toy aisle, pulling her thoughts back to Mary. Hannah's instinct was to buy every toy in the store for the little girl. The life insurance money she'd received following the accident was more than Hannah would ever spend in her lifetime. From the moment she heard about the Matthews family, ideas on how she could help to make this Christmas a happy one for the family swirled in her mind.

Nellie returned ferrying a plate with two fluffy cinnamon rolls covered in a sticky, glistening glaze. She placed the pastries on the counter. "Let me get you some coffee." Nellie worked her way down to the industrial coffee maker. "I like to keep freshly brewed coffee going all day. Many of the local retired men like to stop by in the early afternoon for coffee and a slice of pie. Would you like cream or sugar?"

"Just black, please. There's enough sugar on this plate to keep me running at high speed all day." Hannah swiped her finger along the edge of a roll and took a lick. "Yum…this is heavenly. You're going to join me, right? I can't eat two." Of course, Hannah knew she could.

Nellie poured two cups of coffee and placed them in front of Hannah. She slid onto a stool she kept behind the counter. "I keep this here on days when my arthritis acts up." She took a seat directly across from Hannah. "I'm afraid the days of enjoying my baked goods are behind me. My blood sugar is too high. If you can't finish both, I'll wrap it up so you can take it home."

Hannah picked up the pastry and took a bite. "I've never tasted something so good in my life. You should be selling these to grocery store chains."

"Then it would be a job. I'm happy just baking for the community and out-of-town visitors." Nellie took a sip from her mug. "What did you want to talk with me about?"

After tasting this scrumptious treat, Hannah made a mental note to ask Nellie if she would be interested in setting up a booth at the festival. That discussion could wait. The Matthews family weighed heavily on her mind. "Actually, I wanted to ask you about one of the local families. If you don't feel comfortable answering my questions, just say so. I'll understand."

"One thing you'll learn living in Bluebell Canyon is that our residents don't keep secrets from each other. To outsiders, it might seem like meddling. It's not that we want to be in everyone else's business; it's just our way of staying connected. How can you pray for your friend or neighbor if you don't know their struggles? We encourage one another to share their challenges so we can provide support."

Secrets.

Hannah shivered.

Was she being deceitful for not opening up to Nellie or Cody about her past? She'd left Phoenix in order to start a new life. A life where people didn't know about her loss. A place where friends didn't feel uncomfortable talking about their children because they knew Hannah had lost her only child. "I wondered if you could tell me a little more about Mary Matthews. She's a student in my class. Recently, it came to my attention that her family is going through some tough times."

Nellie's normally happy expression faded. "Yes, poor little Mary. It's been a difficult year for her family. Mary's mother, Joyce, was diagnosed with breast cancer. She's recently started chemotherapy in Denver. Her employer has been kind enough to allow her to work remotely."

Cancer.

The situation was worse than Hannah had expected. Her heart broke for the sweet little girl who was always so attentive and polite in class. After Hannah took over the class, she should have made more of an effort to get to know each student better…particularly their family life. Mary's parents were the only ones who hadn't attended Parents' Night. At the time, Hannah hadn't thought anything about it. Maybe they had another obligation. But Hannah should have made a point of reaching out to the parents to introduce herself and get to know them. "That's so sad to hear."

"Joyce is tough and her faith is strong. What's made it more of a challenge is Joe's recent injury."

"His knee, right?"

Nellie frowned. "Yes, and unfortunately, it's the right knee so he's been unable to drive. Several women from church have been rotating turns driving Joyce to her treatments."

Hannah's first instinct was to add her name into the rotation, but she knew that wasn't possible with her schedule at school. "Is there anything I can do to help?"

"You can pray. Joe is in jeopardy of losing his health insurance if he doesn't get back to work soon."

Hannah shook her head. Knowing one of her students was facing these difficulties broke her heart. "Is Mary an only child?"

"Yes. She was conceived after Joyce had several miscarriages. All of the specialists told her she'd never be able to carry a baby to term."

"Thank you for sharing their situation with me. I appreciate it," Hannah said.

The front door bell rang, filling the silence that hung in the air.

Nellie stood. "That's Nelson. He's coming to take a look at the bathroom sink in the back room. Stay and finish your coffee and rolls." She reached down behind the counter. "Here's a to-go box if you have any leftovers."

"Thank you, but I need to get going." Hannah picked up the partially eaten cinnamon roll and the one that remained untouched. She placed both inside the container. After learning of the challenges facing the Matthews family, Hannah's appetite had ceased, but she was determined to help the family in any way that she could.

Chapter Seven

Cody stood at the pavilion inside the town square, where he had asked Hannah to meet him. Light snowflakes falling from the gray, low-hanging clouds had kicked Ellie's energy level into high gear. "You love the snow, don't you, girl." Cody scratched the top of the dog's head as she appeared to be attempting to catch the flakes with her mouth. While training dogs, it was always a challenge for Cody not to get too attached.

Ellie barked in response.

A glance at his watch told him Hannah was due to arrive any moment. A flutter of nerves rippled through him. Cody was anticipating spending time with Hannah, but the situation seemed to create feelings he wasn't sure he was ready to handle. Lately, when Hannah wasn't around, no matter how hard he tried, she seemed to be all he could think about.

Across the square, Cody observed a young family carrying bags filled with purchases. The two adults laughed while the young boy and girl began a snowball fight. A yearning for a family of his own tugged at his heart. The closer to the date where he could legally file for adoption, the more frequently he envisioned a future with McKenzie and Madison. A few times, Hannah was a part of that daydream. He needed to keep reminding himself of the painful end to his relationship with Mallory. His heart couldn't endure another bad breakup, especially when he needed to keep the twins his top priority. Cody would not let down his best friend.

While Cody tried to force the warm thoughts of Hannah out of his head, he spotted her. His pulse raced as she moved closer. Her presence lit up the square. Her winter coat was unzipped, and underneath she wore a cozy, cream-colored cable-knit sweater along with a red scarf. Her cheeks had a healthy flush from the cold air. Hannah's genuine smile could melt the biggest snowbank into a puddle within seconds.

Once Ellie spotted Hannah, the dog's tail began wagging rapidly. Hannah's presence seemed to have the same effect on Ellie as it did on him. "I know how you feel," Cody addressed Ellie, and gripped the leash tighter.

Hannah reached Cody. Her smile grew more infectious as she knelt to greet Ellie. "Hey there, sweetie. I've missed you," she cooed, her voice warm and affectionate. Hannah gave Ellie a lingering scratch behind the ears, prompting an ecstatic response of sloppy, wet licks to her hand.

Hannah had a way with animals, particularly Ellie. It was one of her many admirable traits that made his attraction to her nearly impossible to deny.

Cody pushed aside his feelings of envy and cleared his throat in hopes of getting a little attention for himself. "Hey, Hannah. I'm here too," he said, trying to keep his voice steady.

She chuckled. "I'm sorry." Hannah looked up from Ellie and met Cody's eyes with a warmth that made his heart pound against his chest. "I got a little carried away saying hello to Ellie. I didn't mean to ignore you."

"Yeah, I know who comes first around here," Cody laughed. "It's obvious Ellie adores you."

Hannah blushed and looked down at Ellie. "Well, the feeling is mutual. How can you not love that face?"

"She is quite the charmer. Once she spotted you, I wasn't sure I'd be able to hold onto the leash without suffering severe burns to my hands," Cody said, smiling. "Anyway, thanks for coming out this morning."

Hannah moved her attention back to Cody. Her expression was now sincere. "Of course. I'm excited to help with Ellie's training. I apologize for being wishy-washy about it initially."

"You're here now. That's all that matters."

Once again, Hannah's smile attempted to steal his train of thought. Cody quickly refocused on the task at hand.

"So what do we do first?" Hannah asked.

Cody admired Hannah's eagerness to get to work. "Our goal for today is to work on Ellie's social skills. Primarily focusing on her ability to handle distractions in public places."

"Have you taken her out much?"

Cody laughed. "A few times, but not since the infamous hot dog caper."

"I can't wait to hear this. What happened?" Hannah tightened the scarf around her neck.

"A few weeks ago, some of the store owners in town were hosting a sidewalk sale. It's something they do periodically to draw visitors into their stores. Anyway, outside of Garrison's Mercantile, Hank was grilling hot dogs for the patrons. He had just taken around ten dogs off the grill and placed the plate on a folding card table when he ran inside for the buns."

"Oh no." Hannah covered her mouth with her hand.

"Yep. Madison had Ellie on the leash, but Madison was busy sampling some of Nellie's homemade peanut butter fudge. She hadn't realized Ellie had devoured every hot dog from the plate until Hank came back outside. At that moment, Ellie spotted a squirrel farther down the sidewalk and took off. Madison lost hold of the leash and Ellie ran down the crowded sidewalk, knocking over displays of merchandise."

Hannah laughed. "I'm sorry. I guess it's not funny."

Cody shook his head. "Actually, it was hilarious. Of course, I didn't let Hank know that's how I felt. You should have seen him chasing after Ellie. I had no idea a guy his age could run so fast. Anyway, since Ellie's going to work as a service dog for those dealing with panic attacks, it's crucial that she remain calm and focused, especially in busy environments filled with distractions. Right now, she's not able to do that. That's what I'd like to work on today."

Hannah gave Cody her full attention. "Where should we start?"

Cody gestured outward. "We'll begin right here. With it being Saturday morning, there are plenty of people out and about running their errands and walking their dogs. There's a plethora of distractions out here to drive Ellie bonkers." He handed the leash over to Hannah.

"You want me to handle her? I'm not sure if I'm ready for that."

Cody couldn't ignore the fear in her eyes. Hannah shifted her weight from side to side. He wasn't sure why she'd have this kind of reaction. During Hannah's past interactions with Ellie, she hadn't exhibited any reluctance. Why now? "I believe you're more than ready. I have total confidence in you. Remember, if she remains calm be sure to acknowledge her as we go along with praise, affection or treats." Cody handed off a couple of bacon bites to Hannah. "Here, put these in your pocket. The positive reinforcement is important."

With Ellie's leash in hand, Hannah led the way.

Cody followed closely enough to inhale her floral scent trailing behind. Perhaps it was Hannah's shampoo. Ellie trotted obediently beside them. Her tail whipped back and forth while she kept her focus on Hannah.

"Good girl, Ellie." Hannah spoke softly to the animal and smiled at Cody.

As they made their way through the square, the air turned colder while the flakes of snow grew larger. A few breaks in the clouds allowed a little blue sky to reveal itself.

"We might see a little sunshine this afternoon," Cody remarked, seeing his breath.

"I sure hope so. It's a little too cold for my liking. Ellie seems to enjoy the snow, though."

Ellie spied a squirrel running toward a birch tree. The dog gave an abrupt yank on the leash, trying to move faster. Hannah held firm.

"Yes, she loves it. She also can't resist squirrels. Continue to keep a tight grip on the leash so she knows you are in control. You're doing great."

Hannah complied and Ellie slowed her pace. "Good girl," Hannah said, praising the animal.

"Having a service dog that's able to stay composed in a crowded and distracting environment is crucial for someone experiencing a panic attack. The dog must maintain their focus on the handler's needs, especially during moments of distress. We want to ensure a sense of comfort and security to the handler."

Hannah listened attentively to Cody's explanation, but stayed quiet.

On the other side of the square, a large group of children played on the swings. Another cluster of boys attempted to build a snowman. With merely a dusting on the ground, the construction soon erupted into a snowball fight, igniting a host of screams along with laughter.

"Let's head over there." Cody pointed to the rambunctious little boys. "It's a bit noisier with all of those children." He extended his hand to take over. "We can introduce some controlled distractions to test Ellie. I'll show you what I mean."

Hannah nodded and released her grip on the leash.

They approached the children. Happy chatter and bursts of laughter filled the air.

Cody slightly increased the speed of their walk. Ellie matched his stride. Cody allowed Ellie to observe the activities going on around her, but he encouraged her to remain focused on him.

"Ellie—watch me." Cody instructed the dog in a calm, but firm tone. He maintained eye contact with Ellie while she followed his lead, keeping her dark eyes locked onto his.

Cody guided Ellie toward a hot dog vendor producing tempting smells. Ellie remained focused on Cody and responded to his commands. "Good girl, Ellie." He patted her head.

Hannah kept a close eye on Cody while he continued to allow Ellie to move through the distractions. Ellie's head moved, taking in her surroundings but not responding to the children shouting.

"Let's have a seat over there." Cody nodded his head in the direction of a bench away from other people.

They took a seat and Cody reached into his pocket for a treat. Ellie sat on the ground at Cody's feet and turned her head up to him. "Good girl." He extended his hand and Ellie gobbled the biscuit.

"You two make a great team. You make it look so easy," Hannah remarked.

Cody was proud of Ellie. She'd come a long way. "Thank you. It's all about building trust and a strong bond with the dog."

"I can see how the training takes a lot of patience and consistency."

"It does, but it's worth it." Cody reached down and scratched Ellie behind the ear. The dog thumped her tail in response. "It's incredible to witness the difference a well-trained service dog can make in someone's life. For people struggling with panic attacks or PTSD, having a reliable and loyal companion like Ellie can provide a sense of security and support that's hard to put into words."

Apart from a nod, Hannah didn't respond. Cody took note of her stiffened posture.

An awkward silence hung in the air. Cody turned and faced Hannah. "I suppose training a dog is much like teaching children."

Hannah tucked a strand of hair behind her ear. "Kind of, I guess."

Something was different about Hannah. He couldn't quite put his finger on it. It seemed her once playful attitude from earlier had disappeared as quickly as a spectacular sunset. "You're so good with kids. Have you ever thought of having any of your own?"

Hannah's stiff posture now seemed to become frozen. Her face turned to stone. "That's kind of a personal question, don't you think?"

Cody was never good at small talk...especially with women. "I'm sorry. I didn't mean to upset you. I thought it was something one friend might ask another. My mistake to assume we're friends now."

Hannah stood up. "I think it's best if we keep our time together focusing on our common goals. To plan a successful festival and allow me to help you train Ellie."

Cody got up to look Hannah square in the eyes. "I'll be totally honest with you. As much as I've tried to deny my feelings, I like you. A lot. It's only natural for me to want to learn more about you. Is that so wrong?"

"I'm sorry." Hannah shook her head. "But I can't do this."

Before Cody had a chance to respond, Hannah took off running across the town square. Her red scarf fell to the ground, but Hannah didn't notice or maybe she didn't care. Ellie jumped to her feet and barked.

Cody wanted to run after Hannah, but it was obvious she wanted to be as far away from him as possible. Regret consumed him. Why had he opened his heart to her? Did he not learn anything from his past relationship?

* * *

The panic attack was bad. Not as bad as the first following the loss of her family, but a close second.

Hannah tried all of her standby methods to get her breathing under control, but nothing worked. At least she was safe inside of her car. Alone. Away from Cody. What must he be thinking? He shared his feelings and she bolted. What choice did she have?

If she had to do it over again, Hannah would have answered Cody's question differently. But it was too late now. Thankfully, Cody hadn't come after her or he would have witnessed the panic attack. Then he'd have even more questions. Her breathing had finally slowed and her hands stopped shaking enough to start her car. It was safe to drive.

Slowly, she backed the SUV from the parking space and headed home. Her safe place. But for how long? It was only a matter of time before she'd have to face Cody. Keeping her past a secret from him was wrong. She knew it. But talking about the horrific accident and what she had lost was too painful.

Monday morning, Hannah stepped inside of the teachers' lounge to grab a quick cup of coffee before class started.

"We missed you in church yesterday, Hannah." Principal Murray looked up from her tablet.

"I was feeling a bit under the weather, but I'm fine now." Rather than face Cody, Hannah had decided to stay home from church. Given her abrupt departure from the town square on Saturday, she wasn't sure if Cody would question her more about having children or anything else personal. He'd admitted he had feelings for her. The truth was that she liked him too. A lot. It would only make sense—given their mutual feelings for each other—that the more time they spent together, she'd be forced to tell him. He deserved to know the truth. But she didn't want him to know about the panic attacks. Cody believed she was a strong, independent woman. Surely his feelings about her would change if he knew the real Hannah.

"I'm glad you're feeling better. Do you have a minute to talk?"

Hannah sat in the empty chair across from the principal. "Of course. What's up?"

"I had a favor to ask of you. I know you and Cody Beckett are organizing the Christmas festival, so you're probably spending a lot of time together."

Hannah's stomach twisted at the mention of Cody's name. His expression when she'd snapped at him on Saturday flashed through her mind. "Sure, I'll try to help. What is it?"

"Since his visit to the school with the service dog, several teachers have suggested regular visits could be beneficial to the students. In particular, students who might have emotional issues or problems they're dealing with at home."

Hannah nodded. Like Mary Matthews. "I agree with you and the other teachers, but I'm not sure where I come into play with this," Hannah remarked.

Principal Murray clasped her hands together and rested them on the table. "I know the Beckett brothers are busy with their business and their families. I thought maybe you'd have a better idea whether this is something Cody would be receptive to or even have the time for. Do you think you could run the idea by Cody and see what he thinks?"

Hannah's shoulders relaxed, relieved it wasn't a favor that would involve her and Cody spending even more time together. Between the festival planning and helping with Ellie, she was seeing him more than any other friends in town. Which wouldn't be an issue, but she wasn't attracted to her other friends. As much as she tried to deny it, her feelings for Cody were growing. "Of course, I can ask him."

"Does it sound like something he'd like to do?" Principal Murray's eyes brightened.

"Actually, I think it's just the kind of service Cody and his brothers enjoy providing to the community. Not to mention the exposure it gives them to show the benefits a service dog can offer."

"That's great to hear."

Hannah nodded. She had been thinking it might be a good idea for them to have a booth at the festival. Hannah had planned to mention it to Cody on Saturday, but she hightailed it out of the town square too quickly. Regret devoured her once she'd reached her car. In hindsight, maybe Saturday was her opportunity to tell him the truth behind her move to Bluebell Canyon. Now, the excitement she'd begun to experience as she looked forward to each new planning session with Cody was marred by a black cloud of dread.

Hannah glanced at the clock on the wall. "I need to head to my classroom. I'll be sure and mention this to Cody the next time I see him."

"Thanks so much." Principal Murray returned her focus to the tablet.

An hour and a half later, Hannah stood from behind the desk. "Children, please pass your homework assignments from last Friday to the front of the class."

The sound of papers shuffling filled the room as the children did as they were asked.

"I'd now like for you to open your arithmetic books to page twenty."

"Stop it!" McKenzie's shout echoed throughout the classroom.

Hannah turned her attention to the commotion in the back of the room.

"Is there a problem, McKenzie?" Hannah noticed the child's face was red. Suzie, the student sitting to her right, had a grip on McKenzie's notebook with no sign of letting go.

"No." McKenzie avoided eye contact, but swatted her hand for Suzie to let go of her book.

"McKenzie didn't do her homework," Suzie announced to the class. She turned to McKenzie and stuck out her tongue.

"Suzie! That's enough. Now, girls, please settle down." Hannah walked out from behind her desk.

"Tell her to give me my notebook!" McKenzie shouted, ignoring Hannah's instructions.

"McKenzie, please stop yelling." Hannah looked at Suzie. "That's not your property. Give it back to McKenzie."

Suzie reluctantly released her grip.

McKenzie jerked it away and stuck out her tongue in turn at Suzie.

"McKenzie—that's enough." Something had the child upset and Hannah wasn't so sure it had anything to do with homework or the notebook. She glanced at her watch. It was a few minutes until recess, but Hannah wanted to get to the bottom of things. "Children, we'll finish the math assignment after recess. Grab your coats and head outside." Hannah looked toward the window and noticed Mrs. Weaver outside with her class. "Mrs. Weaver is in charge until I join you."

Cheers erupted as the kids raced to the coatroom, free to go outdoors. A few of the children giggled and whispered how their classmates were in big trouble.

Hannah moved to the back of the class where McKenzie remained seated. Suzie had left with the other children. "Don't you want to go outside?"

McKenzie chewed on her lip. "Aren't I in trouble? Don't you want to call Uncle Cody?"

"I'd rather discuss this with you and not involve your uncle. He's a busy man." Hannah knew Cody had a hectic schedule, but she had other reasons for not wanting to call him right now.

McKenzie folded her arms and rolled her lower lip. "What if I don't want to talk?"

Hannah wasn't sure what had prompted this sudden behavior change from McKenzie. Yes, she'd had some recent disciplinary issues in class, but up until today, her attitude had improved. She'd been well-mannered and sweet Friday night when the twins and Cody took Hannah on a walking tour in order to brainstorm ideas for the festival. Something had McKenzie upset. Hannah was determined to get to the bottom of the cause. The last thing she wanted was for McKenzie to be in pain. If it meant reaching out to Cody, she'd have to put her own problems aside and do what was best for McKenzie.

"Will you at least tell me why you didn't complete your homework assignment?"

"I didn't want to." McKenzie answered with no hesitation. *Okay. Let's try this again.* "Is there something that's bothering you, sweetie? You know you can always talk to me."

McKenzie kept her lips pursed.

Hannah realized this was a losing battle. "Go and grab your coat. We'll join the rest of the class outside."

"You're not going to call Uncle Cody?"

Hannah had every intention of reaching out to Cody, but she wasn't going to tell McKenzie. It was obviously what the child wanted. This was all part of the girls' matchmaking scheme. McKenzie wanted her teacher to contact her uncle and that was exactly what Hannah planned to do, only she wasn't going to tell McKenzie.

As Hannah slipped on her coat, she reached inside the pocket for her phone. McKenzie raced out the door to head to the playground. Hannah moved down the hallway and shot a quick text message to Cody. Her heart raced as she typed the words. We need to talk.

Chapter Eight

Cody stood in his kitchen and stared at his phone. Only seconds ago, it had chimed an incoming message. He'd forgotten to put in his eye drops that morning, so he rubbed his eyes to make sure he was reading the device correctly. A text from Hannah. His eyes weren't playing tricks on him.

Hannah was the last person he expected to hear from on Monday morning. After she'd abruptly left him standing alone in the middle of the town square Saturday afternoon, he hadn't seen or heard from her since. Yesterday at church, he'd kept his eyes on the door, but there'd been no sign of her. A part of him wanted to reach out to make sure she was okay, but her actions told him it was best to wait it out. He'd made the decision that if and when she wanted to share her past, he'd be ready to listen. Could she be ready now?

Cody responded immediately, knowing she was on a break at school or the kids were at recess.

Name the time and place.

Can you come to my classroom after school? It's McKenzie. We had a problem during class today.

Cody clenched his teeth. He had hoped McKenzie's episodes in class were behind her.

I'll be there. I'll call my sister-in-law and ask her to pick up Madison, unless you need her to stay as well?

No, only McKenzie. See you then.

Later that day, Cody and Logan returned from Denver after picking up two rescue pups from a shelter. The Labrador retrievers—both from the same litter—were found abandoned on a construction site. During the road trip, Cody's mind was preoccupied with his meeting at the school. Since Logan planned to pick up Henry from school, he offered to take Madison back to his house.

With Hannah's red scarf in his hand, Cody's heartbeat pounded as he stepped inside of the classroom. He spotted Hannah and McKenzie sitting at the craft table.

"Uncle Cody!" McKenzie sprang from the chair and met him halfway. "I was afraid you weren't coming." She flung her arms around his waist.

Cody stroked the top of McKenzie's head. "I'll always be here for you. I hope you know that."

McKenzie nodded. "Maybe the three of us can all go to the Hummingbird Café for some hot chocolate."

Cody glanced at Hannah, who remained at the table. He looked down at McKenzie. "I'm afraid we can't do that today. Miss Simpson called me here because of your behavior in class this morning."

"Oh…well that was nothing." McKenzie chewed on the side of her lower lip.

"Let's all sit down together so Miss Simpson can fill me in on what happened." Cody took McKenzie's hand and guided her back to the table where Hannah waited. They both took a seat across from Hannah.

Cody passed the scarf across the table. "You dropped this the other day."

Hannah reached for the scarf. Her face blushed when their fingers brushed. "Thank you."

Cody pulled his attention away from Hannah and focused on McKenzie. "Do you want to tell me why Miss Simpson called me here?"

"I didn't do my homework," McKenzie blurted out. "But I'll do it tonight. I'll even do extra. Can we go get hot chocolate now?"

Cody shook his head. "Let Miss Simpson speak."

Hannah explained to Cody exactly what had transpired earlier in the day regarding McKenzie's homework. She went on to inform him about the disruption in the classroom between McKenzie and Suzie.

Cody addressed McKenzie. "Can you tell us why you didn't do your homework? If the assignment was given on Friday, you had all weekend to do it."

McKenzie rolled her shoulders. "I don't know."

"That's not a good enough reason." Cody looked over to Hannah. "Did Madison complete her assignment?"

"Yes, she did. She even did a couple extra problems. I think she enjoys math."

McKenzie rolled her eyes. "I had more stuff to do than she did."

Cody cleared his throat. "Since you don't have a good reason for not doing your homework, I'm afraid you'll have to be grounded. No more helping with Ellie's training or any care for the dogs. It's obviously more than you can handle and interfering with your studies."

"That's not fair!"

"McKenzie, please lower your voice. What's not fair is you disrupting Miss Simpson's class. Not to mention how disrespectful it is of you not to have your assignments completed on time." Cody's face warmed. "Unless you can give me a better reason why you didn't do your homework, but Madison did hers, you're leaving me no choice but to punish you."

McKenzie's lip quivered. "But I like helping with the dogs."

Hannah and Cody exchanged looks.

Cody folded his arms across his chest. "What if I tell you why I think you didn't do your homework. Will you tell me if I'm right?"

McKenzie shifted her eyes to the table then back to Cody. "Okay."

"I think you didn't do your math because you wanted to get into trouble."

McKenzie squirmed, but remained quiet.

"You tell me if I'm wrong. It seems since Miss Simpson became your teacher, you went from being a model student to one who acts out, creates disruptions in the classroom and now, not completing your assignments. Do you think that's a good observation?" Cody waited for her response and expected her to agree.

What he didn't expect was his heart to break. McKenzie burst into tears, something he'd never seen her do. Madison was the twin who showed her emotions easily, especially when it came to losing her father. McKenzie was the complete opposite. She portrayed a tough-as-nails front, until now.

Guilt settled deep inside Cody. Had he pushed her too hard? Raising children—this was all new to him.

McKenzie's lip quivered as she struggled to speak. "Saturday night when me and Madison were watching a movie, I overheard you on the phone with Uncle Jake," McKenzie said through her tears. "You said Miss Simpson ran away from you, but you didn't know why."

Hannah placed her elbows on the table and covered her mouth. A group of teachers laughed outside the classroom as they walked by.

"It's not polite to listen to other people's conversations,"

Cody said, mainly in an attempt to buy time to try and recall exactly what McKenzie might have overheard.

"I wasn't doing it on purpose. I just could hear you." McKenzie wiped her eyes, yet the tears continued. "You told Uncle Jake you didn't think you and Miss Simpson could keep working together on the festival."

From what Cody could remember of the conversation with his brother, McKenzie had tuned in toward the end of the phone call. Thankfully, she hadn't heard the entire discussion. McKenzie didn't hear him tell Jake he was falling for Hannah. That was a relief. That tidbit of information would only increase the twins' matchmaking endeavors.

"If you can't work together, you'll never—"

Hannah turned to Cody, as though looking for him to finish McKenzie's sentence. He shrugged his shoulders.

"We'll never what?" Cody rested his hand on McKenzie's arm.

"You'll never go on a real date and fall in love."

Cody noticed Hannah's eyes widen before she gave him an understanding nod.

Their suspicions were confirmed. There had been a motive behind McKenzie's disruptive behavior. "So you've been trying to bring your teacher and I together by getting in trouble on purpose?"

McKenzie nodded. "If you don't fall in love, you won't ask Miss Simpson to marry you."

"But that doesn't mean we can't be friends. Your teacher and I can resolve any differences we have and continue working together to plan the festival. You don't need to worry yourself sick about it."

"I don't want you to be friends. I want you to get married! If you don't, me and Madison will never be part of a family again." McKenzie spoke loud enough that anyone passing the classroom door could have heard the outburst.

McKenzie faced her teacher. "Don't you like Uncle Cody? I don't want you to fight."

"May I?" Hannah directed her question to Cody.

"Yes, please do." Cody wasn't sure how this had snow-balled. But then again, he was spending a lot of time with Hannah between the festival planning and training Ellie to-gether. Were he and Hannah to blame in giving McKenzie false hope and sending mixed messages that there was more to their relationship?

Hannah stood and moved to the empty chair on the other side of McKenzie. "Sweetie, I don't want you to be upset. Your uncle and I aren't fighting. My actions on Saturday were wrong. I should have never run off like I did." She glanced at Cody. "I have every intention of explaining myself very soon."

"Then why can't you be boyfriend and girlfriend so you can get married?"

"Well, for one reason, we hardly know each other. Marriage isn't something to take lightly. It takes time for two people to build a relationship," Hannah explained.

"But we don't have time!" McKenzie hit her hand on the table.

"McKenzie, please lower your voice." The last thing Cody wanted was for anyone outside in the hall to overhear the conversation. "Can you explain to us what you mean? There's not enough time for what?"

"If you don't get married soon, you won't be able to adopt me and Madison."

Cody hadn't talked openly to the twins about legally adopt-ing. With all of the self-doubt he'd experienced, he thought it was best to wait until he made a decision. "Where did you hear that?"

"Suzie and Rebecca. They said kids can't be adopted unless there's a mommy and daddy. Suzie said judges only give kids to families." McKenzie wiped her eyes. "Me and Madison are going to end up in some place filled with kids nobody wants."

Cody's stomach turned over at the pain in McKenzie's eyes. He was the reason she was so distraught. He rose from his chair and crouched in front of McKenzie. He took hold of both her hands and squeezed his eyes shut in an attempt to hide his own tears. "What your friends told you isn't true."

"Why would they say that?" McKenzie's forehead crinkled.

"I'm not sure I have an answer for you, sweetie. Sometimes people say things without thinking how it will make the other person feel. Suzie and Rebecca were wrong to say those things to you, but I was wrong, too."

McKenzie shifted in her chair. "I thought grown-ups were always right."

Cody squeezed McKenzie's hands a little tighter. "We can mess up just like kids can. No one is perfect." He drew in a breath and held it before releasing. "I should have talked with you and your sister about the adoption process."

"Do you not want us?"

Cody dropped his chin to his chest and shook his head. This was not what his best friend had wanted for his girls when he'd entrusted Cody as their guardian. Cody wanted nothing more than to fulfill his friend's last wishes. He just wasn't sure if he was capable. "I think I want you both more than I even realized. In fact, I know I want you both—very much. But lately, I've allowed fear to fill my heart."

"You're afraid? But you're so big and strong."

Out of the mouth of babes. Cody had so much to learn about children. It was then he realized there were a lot of things he could teach McKenzie and Madison, starting with the fact that it's okay to admit when you're scared. "Yes, I am afraid. I'm afraid of disappointing your father. But I'm more scared that I'm not qualified to fill his shoes. There's not much I know about raising two little girls. What if I mess it up?"

"It's okay if you do. We'll still love you." McKenzie smiled.

Cody opened his arms and McKenzie lunged from the chair. With his arms tightly around her, Cody pressed his face against her shoulder, unable to hold back his tears. A sense of strength and confidence that had been absent rushed through his body. He could do this. It was what he wanted—to be a family. Cody made a promise to himself and God he would spend the rest of his life making sure McKenzie and Madison felt safe and loved.

Thursday afternoon, Hannah arrived at the mayor's office. Since Jennifer, the receptionist, wasn't at her desk, Hannah took a seat in the empty reception area. Last night, the mayor sent an email to her and Cody asking them to stop by today for an emergency meeting. Hannah came over right after school, knowing she'd be early.

Since receiving the email, Hannah was apprehensive about the meeting. Her first instinct had been to call Cody to see if he had any idea what had prompted the mayor to call them to his office. But after what had transpired last weekend at the town square, she decided against it. Of course, that hadn't been the only reason she held back.

Earlier in the week, following the touching scene that unfolded in her classroom between Cody and McKenzie, Hannah had fallen for Cody just a little more. As the scene replayed in her mind, she had to admit to herself she'd fallen more than a little. The love he showed to McKenzie about the impending adoption reinforced everything Hannah believed about Cody. He would make a wonderful father. There was no reason in the world he should question his ability.

The front entrance door pushed open, pulling Hannah from her thoughts and ushering in a blast of arctic air, along with some wispy snowflakes. She turned and the cold air was instantly replaced with heat when she spotted Cody. Wearing his black Stetson, dark leather jacket and well-worn jeans, he stole her breath away.

"Man, it's cold outside," Cody said to himself while he stomped his feet on the doormat and removed his hat, unaware of her presence.

"The weatherman said a storm is moving in from the west," Hannah said in a low tone.

Cody smiled. "Sorry, I didn't see you when I first came in. I think my eyelids were frozen shut. The temperature has really dropped from early today. If this keeps up, the roads are going to get a little dicey." He peeled off his jacket and hung it on the corner rack. "Have you seen the mayor?"

"Not yet. I heard his voice in his office so I think he's on the phone." Hannah stood and walked over to the watercooler to refill her cup. "Would you like some water?" she offered.

"I'd rather have something hot to drink, but I guess that will have to do."

Hannah would like nothing more than to blow off the meeting with the mayor and head over to the Hummingbird Café. With the weather conditions deteriorating outside, it was the perfect time to enjoy a hot chocolate while sitting by the fire. She shook off the thought when Cody appeared in her daydream. Not exactly the way to keep things all business.

Hannah got Cody's water and moved back to her chair, where he'd taken a seat beside her.

"Thanks." He took the cup and drank the contents down in one long gulp.

Despite seeing each other in the classroom on Monday, the awkwardness remained now that they were alone. But any attempt to clear the air today would have to wait. After Cody declared he had feelings for Hannah and she had admitted to herself the feeling was mutual, she realized their relationship could head into a different direction. Was that something she was ready for?

"I'm sorry to keep you two waiting." Mayor Jennings exited his office and joined his guests in the reception area. "Let me grab some water. Please, feel free to go ahead and take a seat at the round table. I'll be right with you." The mayor motioned toward his office.

Hannah gathered her notebook and a few pieces of paper from the coffee table. Cody moved across the room while silencing his phone before slipping it into his back pocket.

Inside the mayor's office, Hannah sat down at the table. Cody took the empty seat next to her.

Mayor Jennings entered the room and closed the door behind him. He walked over to his desk, grabbed his tablet and joined Hannah and Cody. "Thank you both for coming today."

"Your email sounded urgent," Cody stated.

Hannah tapped her finger nervously along the side of her notebook. She sensed a somber tone in the mayor's greeting. She didn't have a good feeling about this.

The mayor leaned forward, clasped his fingers together and rested his hands on the massive cherrywood conference table. His expressive was grave. "I'll get right to the point. Last night, the budget committee held an emergency meeting after receiving quotes from several road crews who'd put in a bid to repair Old Keene Mill Road." He directed his attention to Hannah. "Cody is aware of what happened last spring, but being a newer resident, you might not have heard about it. Last April, we had experienced torrential flooding that washed out a large portion of the highway. The road is impassible so it's been closed. Unfortunately, the bids we received were all higher than anticipated, creating significant budgetary challenges."

"This can't be good." Cody shook his head.

"I'm sorry to be the bearer of bad news, but these challenges will directly impact the town's annual Christmas festival. The committee had to make the cuts from somewhere.

The festival seemed like the most logical place. I know this isn't what you want to hear, but the town's priorities had to be reevaluated. Difficult decisions had to be made in order to address our financial challenges."

Hannah's heart sank as she listened to the mayor. Planning a successful festival for the town of Bluebell Canyon had been her connection to the family she had lost. How could she survive the holidays if she didn't have the preparations to focus on?

Cody cleared his throat. "How exactly will these cuts affect our plans for the festival? We've already lined up sponsors and vendors, not to mention the numerous people who have volunteered their time. This year, Hannah and I had hoped to make the festival the best one the town has ever experienced."

Hannah was relieved Cody was on the same page as her. Perhaps he had his own reasons for planning the festival that were equally as important? In fact, they were quite similar. It came down to family.

Mayor Jennings nodded and looked down at his tablet for a moment. "I appreciate all of the hard work and effort both of you have put into planning this year's festival. I know how much it means to our community. I'm not saying the committee has pulled all of the funds, but it will be substantially less than in years past, so you'll have to make some adjustments."

"As Cody mentioned, creating a memorable festival for the town is important to both of us." Hannah glanced at Cody and he tipped his chin in agreement. "Is there any way the committee can explore alternatives or find additional funding within the budget to mitigate the impact?"

"From what I understand, the members shuffled the money as much as they could without sacrificing necessary expenditures. The best I can do is leave it up to you two to determine which planned events and activities will have to be cut or at least scaled back."

Hannah's mind raced as she considered the mayor's words. "We certainly understand the importance of fiscal responsibility for the town." She looked at Cody again. "We'll just have to brainstorm more ideas to handle this setback."

Cody nodded. "We can continue to reach out to more local sponsors to try and secure more support. If we're successful, maybe we could maintain our original vision. It might not be easy, but we'll find a way. Mr. Mayor, are you able to provide us with specific figures or limits we need to work within?"

The mayor reached into a folder on the table next to him and produced a document, sliding it in front of Hannah and Cody. "This is what the committee came up with."

Hannah scanned the numbers and her heart sank further with each line on the page. The cuts were deep. "It looks like a big reduction in the allocation for entertainment, lights and some of the bigger attractions."

"Yes, that's true. Unfortunately, I'm afraid the fireworks show on the last night of the festival will probably have to be canceled. That's a big expense," the mayor explained.

"But the fireworks are one of the most enjoyed attractions. Even our elderly townspeople stay up later than usual to enjoy them," Cody said.

Hannah couldn't ignore the distraught look on Cody's face. He knew the town better than she did. She took a deep breath before speaking. "We understand the gravity of the town's financial situation. I'm confident Cody and I will be able to revise our current plans accordingly and ensure the festival remains a special event for the town."

Cody gave a slight nod. The disappointment in his eyes remained. "We'll get to work immediately and present you with a revised proposal."

Mayor Jennings offered a reassuring smile. "Given the time constraints, I don't think submitting an amended proposal will be necessary. You both have seen the figures so you know the funds available to you. As I mentioned earlier, I trust you to decide what's best to cut but still bring the holiday spirit to our town."

They shook hands and said goodbye to the mayor.

Alone in the reception area with Hannah, Cody rubbed his hand across his eyes. "I'm not sure how we're going to pull this off."

Hannah put on her coat and shouldered her bag. Cody grabbed his jacket. His disappointment was palpable. Giving McKenzie and Madison a memorable Christmas was just as important to him as it was to her. Only for different reasons she couldn't share with Cody.

They stepped outside into the crisp winter air and exchanged glances. Hannah felt a tingle of excitement. She had a plan to save the festival, but she'd have to do it on her own. Involving Cody would mean revealing her past, something she wasn't ready to do.

Hannah stopped and turned to Cody. "Extraordinary events happen all of the time, especially during the holiday season. We only need to believe."

Chapter Nine

❦

"Can we get the Christmas tree this weekend? They are already selling them in town," McKenzie asked as she took another bite of her waffle. "Today is the first day of December." She pointed to the magnetic calendar hanging on the refrigerator door.

After Thanksgiving, the girls had begun the Christmas countdown. At the end of each day, they marked a big red *X* on the calendar.

Shortly after the twins had come to live with him, Cody had been introduced to the lifesaving world of frozen waffles, thanks to his amazing sister-in-law, Olivia. Mornings like today, when they were running late for school, having the ability to toast waffles and smear them with peanut butter, along with a touch of syrup, had saved Cody a lot of time. "Actually, I had a little surprise for you girls."

McKenzie and Madison's eyes widened as they exchanged quick glances before looking back at Cody.

"What is it?" McKenzie bounced in her chair.

"Yeah, please tell us. We love surprises!" Madison chimed in.

Cody picked up his coffee mug and took a sip, prolonging the girls' curiosity. It made his heart happy to see the twins excited. Since it was their first Christmas without their father, Cody wasn't sure how to approach the holiday, so he'd made the decision to follow their lead. "Early this morning, while I was outside walking Hershey, I had the idea that maybe we'd go out into the woods and cut down our own tree instead of buying one in town. Is that something you'd like to do?"

"Yes!" the girls cheered in unison.

"Like Uncle Logan did last weekend? Henry told us they cut down a huge one!" McKenzie's eyes were like saucers.

Cody and his brother had been known to try and one-up the other. "Yes, but I thought maybe we'd try and get an even bigger tree."

"Cool! Let's get one that reaches the ceiling," Madison exclaimed.

"Well, we have to leave enough room to put the star on top," Cody laughed.

"Can I put it on?" Madison asked.

McKenzie nudged her sister. "No, I want to!"

Cody hadn't thought the girls would argue over the decorations. "Maybe we can get two trees. One for the family room and another for the living room. That way you can each place the star on top."

"Our own tree? That's awesome!" McKenzie cheered.

Madison placed a finger under her chin. "I think I want to put an angel on top of mine."

Cody's shoulders relaxed. His quick thinking had put an end to the disagreement between the twins. He hadn't considered having two trees, but why not? Maybe he knew more about parenting than he gave himself credit for. "You can each decorate your tree the way you want to."

"So can we go tomorrow?" McKenzie asked.

"Under one condition."

"What?" they asked at the same time.

"You run upstairs and brush your teeth, so we can leave for school in the next ten minutes."

Silverware clinked against the plates as the twins dropped

their forks and jumped out of their chairs. "We'll be right back," McKenzie promised.

"I can't believe we get our own tree!" Madison shouted as they raced from the kitchen.

Cody was pleased with his decision. Growing up, his parents always had two Christmas trees in the house during the holidays. Why not continue the tradition?

While clearing the dishes off the table, Cody's phone on the counter chimed, signaling a calendar event. He glanced at the screen reminding him of the ten-thirty meeting scheduled this morning with a vendor in Denver to work out a deal for half a dozen booth rentals.

Yesterday, after learning about the budget cuts, Cody and Hannah had made an agreement. In order to save time, they'd split up and meet with potential volunteers and participants to complete the planning for the festival on time. The clock was ticking.

"Let's get going, girls," Cody called from downstairs. He needed to get to the school soon in order to make his meeting on time.

Later in the day, Cody stepped inside of Garrison's Mercantile to pick up some popcorn and soda. Sugary beverages weren't something he normally allowed the girls to have, but tonight was a special evening before their big Christmas tree search in the morning. Since he didn't want them bouncing off the walls come bedtime, he opted for caffeine-free soda.

"Good afternoon, Cody." Nellie rounded the counter and headed in his direction.

He tossed the box of popcorn into the basket. "Hey, Nellie. How are you and Hank doing?"

"We're fine. Hank just took a large order of groceries over to the Matthews' place."

Cody was relieved to hear that the Matthews wouldn't have to worry about keeping food on their table. Cody had been praying for the family since Joyce's cancer diagnosis and Joe's knee injury.

"It was the strangest thing." Nellie placed her hand to the side of her cheek.

"What's that?"

"Well, when I arrived at the store this morning, I found an envelope underneath the door. It was a handwritten note with instructions to send the necessary grocery items and any other necessities to the Matthews' home. We don't know who requested this."

Cody wasn't surprised by the kind gesture. Bluebell Canyon was filled with generous people. "It shouldn't be hard to figure out if they left a credit card number to cover the cost."

"That's just it. They paid in cash—a lot of cash." Nellie's eyes widened.

"How much are you talking about?"

Nellie looked around the empty store. "I probably shouldn't be sharing this with you, but I can trust you to keep it between us, right?"

Cody nodded. "Of course you can." If there was one thing Cody didn't like, it was someone who wasn't true to their word.

"The person left twenty brand-new one-hundred-dollar bills."

Whoa. True, the town was generous, but most were of smaller means. An amount of money that large would not be easy for most living in town. "Any idea who it could be?" Cody asked.

Nellie shook her head. "Not a clue, but Joe would really like to find out who this kindhearted person is. When Hank called to tell him he was bringing the gift and what it entailed, Joe was speechless. He's so grateful. He wants to thank the person face-to-face, but he doesn't know who it could be either."

"Obviously the person has their reasons for remaining anonymous. I suppose we have to respect that."

"Well, yes," Nellie agreed. "But aren't you dying to know

who it could be? I sure wish Hank had installed that security camera out front like I asked."

Last summer, when some kids were going around town doing a few harmless pranks, most likely out of boredom, Nellie had suggested to her husband that he monitor the storefront. Hank refused to put up a security camera, saying he'd lived in the town his entire life and had never experienced any trouble.

Cody laughed. "I guess you could always stay up all night and watch the door."

"Smart aleck." She rolled her eyes. "You're right, we should be thankful we live in a town that has such generous people. Take you and Hannah, for example. You're donating your time to plan the festival. I know how busy you two are. I can speak for the entire town when I say we appreciate what you're doing."

"There's nothing more I'd rather do with my spare time. I'm sure you heard about the budget cuts for the festival." Of course that was a silly question. Cody was well aware that Nellie usually knew everything that happened in town. That's probably why not knowing who made the anonymous donation was driving her up the wall.

"Yes, but I'm sure you and Hannah will figure things out. She's working hard for the town. In fact, she was out in front of the store early this morning before we even opened."

That seemed odd to Cody, with it being a school day. "What was she doing?"

"Actually, when I first spotted her she was leaving and walking down the front steps. Maybe she forgot our store hours or something. I called out to her and she came back inside to talk with me about renting a booth for the festival."

Cody's earlier meeting in Denver was a success. The vendor agreed to donate fifteen booths in exchange for free advertising by sharing his company name on each booth. Cody had known the guy for several years. He'd contacted Beckett's Canine Training after his granddaughter struggled with epileptic seizures.

"Are you interested in renting a booth?" Cody asked Nellie.

"Hannah is convinced my cinnamon rolls would be a top seller and they could drive out-of-town visitors into the mercantile."

Cody rubbed his stomach. "She's right about your rolls. They are the best I've ever had. Your fudge brownies are fantastic, too. So can we sign you up?"

"I reserved my booth this morning. Not only is Hannah beautiful, she's got a knack for sales." Nellie winked.

He couldn't argue with Nellie's observation about Hannah's looks. In fact, lately it was becoming more of a challenge to keep his eyes off of her and on the festival planning. "That's great. If you know of anyone else who might be interested in a booth, please spread the word."

"I've already spoken with several women from the church circle. I gave them Hannah's number to call with their reservations. They're excited to offer their holiday crafts at the festival. It's a great idea and something that hasn't been done in years past."

Cody couldn't take the credit. "That was all Hannah's idea. I agree with you. It will be a fantastic addition." Cody glanced at his watch. School would be dismissed soon. "I need to pay for this and head over to pick up the girls."

Nellie moved toward the register. "Is this all you need?"

Cody placed the soda and popcorn on the counter. "Yeah, we're having movie night tonight." He slid his wallet from his back pocket.

"That sounds like fun." Nellie rang the items up on the cash register and accepted the cash. "You're so good to them. Your friend made the right decision when he chose you to be their guardian."

Cody released a deep sigh. He hoped Nellie was right.

When it came to the girls, his confidence level was still on shaky ground. "Since we're going out in the morning to get our Christmas trees, I thought tonight would be a good night to watch a couple holiday movies." Cody tossed the change Nellie handed back to him into the donation jar on the counter.

"Did you say *trees*?"

Cody laughed. "That's right. McKenzie and Madison got into a little disagreement about who would be the one to place the star on top of the tree. Then Madison said she wanted an angel instead. I thought, why not have two trees. That's what my parents did when I was growing up."

Nellie placed her hand on her chest. "It's good you're sharing some of your family traditions with them. It's something they'll carry with them for the rest of their lives."

"That's why I'm taking them out to each pick a fresh tree. Growing up, my father always took us out into the woods. We never bought a tree from a lot." Cody still remembered the feeling he had the first time his father let him use the saw by himself. It took a while to cut it down, but once they had it home and decorated, Cody had been proud of himself. He could only hope to recapture that feeling by giving the girls a Christmas to remember.

Ten minutes later, with the treats for movie night stowed in the truck, Cody headed down the hallway to Hannah's classroom. He wanted to let her know about the deal he'd scored with the booths. He also owed her a thank you for taking the lead and getting Nellie to commit to participating. With Nellie onboard, she'll have all of the ladies from church reserving every booth by the end of the day.

Cody peeked his head inside of the classroom and was surprised to see Hannah alone at her desk. He knocked softly so he wouldn't startle her. "Hey, may I come in?"

Hannah smiled as she pushed away from the paperwork. "Hi. Of course, please." She motioned him inside. "On Friday afternoons the kids are always bouncing off the walls, so I send them out to the playground until the final bell rings. You can go pick up the girls, if you're ready to take them home."

"Actually, I was hoping to speak with you alone, if you have a moment." He slid his hands into the pockets of his down vest.

"Sure, I actually planned on texting you later, so in person is better."

Cody assumed she intended to tell him about her conversation with Nellie. He liked that Hannah was holding up her end of their agreement to keep each other up-to-date on the festival plans. "I saw Nellie a few minutes ago and she told me you got her to commit to a booth. Great work. She's already talked to some other ladies from church."

"That's good to hear." Hannah leaned against the desk. "How did your meeting go in Denver this morning?"

"Better than I had hoped. My friend has offered over a dozen of his booths at no charge. He's got more if we need them. At the rate Nellie is spreading the word we might have to take him up on his offer."

"There's a few teachers I plan to speak with as well, so you might be right."

Cody stepped a little closer. "I think your suggestion is going to be a hit. With the money we're going to save by not having to rent the booths, maybe we can have the fireworks show after all."

Hannah smiled. "I suppose we'll have to do some more number crunching before we make that call."

"Probably so. Well, I better head out and get the girls. We're having movie night this evening. I plan to surprise them with a pizza at Mr. Pepperoni on our way home." Cody turned and started toward the door.

"Wait—what I planned to text you about," Hannah called out.

Cody stopped in his tracks. He'd assumed Hannah only

wanted to tell him about Nellie's commitment. Apparently there was something more on her mind. "Oh, right."

She moved closer with a smile that ignited a warm and fuzzy feeling. "I wanted to say thank you for including me in your Christmas tree search tomorrow. I've always wanted to cut down my own tree. That was nice of you to invite me to join you and the twins."

This was news to Cody. He wasn't quite sure how to respond.

"Oh…uh…it wasn't your idea." Hannah crossed her arms and shook her head.

Cody wasn't able to hide his surprise. Was that disappointment he saw in her eyes? Hannah's smile faded and now she appeared wounded. As much as he didn't like the twins extending an invitation without his permission, he couldn't stand seeing Hannah upset. "Actually, I planned on asking you, but it looks like our little matchmakers beat me to it," he laughed.

Following a restless night spent tossing and turning, Hannah was in need of some seriously strong coffee before making any decision on what to wear today. Maybe she should have declined the twins' offer. That was a moot point now.

Since early this morning, Hannah had replayed the surprised look on Cody's face. Yesterday when she thanked him for inviting her to join them on their outing today, it was clear he had no idea that McKenzie and Madison had taken it upon themselves to extend an invitation. They were determined to play matchmaker.

Dressed in her candy cane flannel pajamas and a cup of hot coffee warming her hands, Hannah scanned her walk-in closet with hopes that something would stand out. Since she'd never cut down her own Christmas tree, she wasn't quite sure of the proper attire. With a light snow in the forecast for today, it only made sense that a pair of her favorite jeans, a thick cable-knit sweater, along with her fleece-lined boots were in order.

Keep it simple.

Why was she so concerned about her outfit, anyway?

By the time Hannah arrived at Cody's house, her windshield wipers were fighting a losing battle to keep up with the falling precipitation. The light snow prediction was way off the mark. It was near whiteout conditions as she put her SUV in Park, unfastened the seat belt and carefully made her way up the front steps of the porch.

"She's here, she's here!"

Outside the front door, Hannah heard the excited voices along with the footsteps running through the house. Before she had a chance to knock, the door swung open to reveal the twins' smiling faces.

"Hi Miss Simpson! Isn't it cool it's snowing?" McKenzie's eyes sparkled as though it was Christmas morning.

"Hi girls. I thought you'd be enjoying the snow." Hannah stomped her boots to knock off the icy clumps stuck to the heels.

"Good morning." Cody appeared at the door dressed in jeans along with a red-and-black-checkered flannel shirt.

Hannah's pulse quickened as their eyes connected, igniting a warmth through her entire body. Maybe it was a good thing the snow was coming down so hard. She desperately needed a cooldown, but his handsome good looks were making that impossible at the moment.

"Please, come inside out of the cold. I have a fire going in the family room. We can get you warmed up while the girls finish their breakfast." Cody motioned her inside. "I'll take your coat."

Hannah kept the fact that she was already warmed up to herself. She slipped off her outerwear and shook off the melted snowflakes over the front mat. "It's really coming down out there. Before I left the house, the local weatherman said only light snow this morning."

"Yeah, they can't seem to get it right lately. The storm they predicted the other day never materialized, but this looks like it could result in measurable snow."

"I hope it becomes a blizzard! Then Miss Simpson will have to stay here with us." McKenzie danced around the foyer.

"Yeah, that would be so cool." Madison joined her sister in a snow dance as they worked their way back inside the kitchen to finish their waffles.

Hannah rubbed her hands up and down her arms and glanced at Cody. "It won't be that bad, will it?"

"At this point, I'm not sure. But don't worry. If it gets too treacherous and you don't feel safe driving home, I can take you back. My truck does well in the snow."

Hannah's shoulders relaxed. It had been a long time since she'd felt comforted by a man's words. Cody made her feel protected. It felt nice.

"Follow me." Cody moved to the family room.

Hannah followed behind, observing the home. Despite the high ceilings with dark wooden beams overhead, the large space felt welcoming with its rustic charm. The fireplace emitted a warmth that had Hannah envisioning a cozy day hunkered by the fire, drinking hot chocolate and reading a good book.

"Have a seat by the fire. I'll get you a cup of coffee." Cody disappeared into the kitchen.

Hannah took a seat in the leather recliner closest to the crackling fire, which casted a warm glow through the room and a feeling of safety from the harsh elements outside the bay window. The scent of burnt wood reminded her of visits to her grandmother's when she was a little girl. Christmas was always spent at her mamaw's cozy cabin tucked away in the mountains of West Virginia.

"Here we go." Cody returned carrying a steaming mug of coffee. The rich aroma immediately tickled her senses. She'd been so nervous getting ready, Hannah left half of her coffee on the bathroom vanity untouched.

"Thank you." She met Cody's eyes with a genuine smile.

He settled into an adjacent armchair and released a sigh. "The girls are just about finished with breakfast. They've been a handful this morning."

Hannah's heart fluttered when the flames from the fireplace highlighted the crinkles surrounding his eyes when he smiled. "It's the snow. I've learned over the years it's practically impossible to get a child to focus on anything when it's snowing."

Cody laughed. "That's definitely part of the reason, but they're most excited because you're spending the day with us." He turned to the fire before looking back. "I'm just as excited."

Despite the warmth from the fire, a shiver traveled through Hannah, catching her off guard. "If we're being honest, I couldn't even finish my coffee this morning because my stomach was turned upside down worrying that I'd choose the wrong outfit."

Cody's eyes started at her feet and moved up until his gaze connected with her own. "Trust me, you didn't pick out the wrong outfit."

The popping and crackling of the fire filled the room as Hannah's palms moistened. She couldn't recall the last time she felt this way—like a teenage girl with her first crush. "Well, now I don't think I can finish this cup of coffee." She smiled, excited for what the day might bring.

Chapter Ten

Cody led the way through the woods on his property, keeping a close eye on the twins, who walked Hershey and Ellie on their leashes. Cody had a closer eye on Hannah. Since her arrival, he couldn't stop looking at her. She looked stunning. "Are you okay?" He turned to Hannah, whose teeth chattered, but she wore a smile.

The twins were chatterboxes since they'd left the house on their adventure. Their excitement for the season was contagious.

The heavy snow from earlier now transformed into gentle, wispy flakes. Yet the dark skies above hinted this was merely a lull.

"Oh yes." Hannah's blue eyes locked with his and she grinned. Her breath was visible in the cold air. "It's been a long time since I've enjoyed a hike in the woods. I feel like I'm in a winter wonderland. The smell of pine is wonderful." She secured her scarf tighter around her neck "I can't believe you and your family own this gorgeous land."

Snowflakes caught in her hair, but Hannah didn't seem to care. Cody was entranced by her enthusiasm and playful mood. He found himself fighting feelings he didn't want to have. Well—maybe he did, but he probably shouldn't. No matter how much he longed to walk hand in hand along the snowy path with Hannah, that desire needed to remain tucked deep within his heart.

"You should have worn a hat, Miss Simpson!" Madison pointed to Hannah's head. "Your pretty hair is getting wet from the snowflakes."

Hannah ran her hand down the back of her hair. "You're right. I was in such a hurry this morning, I completely forgot."

Cody reached around and removed the canvas backpack containing the tools needed to cut down the trees from his shoulder. He gave the zipper a yank and pulled out a yellow Beckett's Canine Training baseball cap. "Here, put this on." He passed it to Hannah.

Hannah studied the cap and smiled. "A little shameless advertising—I like that." She brushed the snow from her hair before placing the hat on her head. "How does it look?" She struck a pose.

He was quickly losing the battle against his feelings. Cody swallowed the lump in his throat. The yellow ignited the blue in her eyes, causing his heart to pound against his chest. "I might need to hire you to walk around town wearing that."

"Now you're ready to find the perfect tree!" Madison sang.

Cody pointed to the majestic pine trees adorning the top of the hill. "Let's head up there and start looking."

The twins cheered. "Yeah, this is the best part, Miss Simpson!" McKenzie gave Hannah's hand a quick tug before turning to Madison. "I'll race you to the top!" She took off with Hershey.

"Winner gets to cut down the first tree!" Madison called out, chasing her sister with Ellie running along her side.

Cody stole glances at Hannah while they scaled the hill. The snowfall began to pick up in intensity.

"Look at that." Hannah stopped in her tracks and pointed.

Cody turned and spotted what had caught Hannah's attention. A male cardinal perched on a nearby snow-covered pine tree branch. "If we wait a second, I'm sure his mate is around."

They stood side by side in the hushed winter landscape.

Seconds later, as Cody predicted, the female flew in and settled next to her partner.

"They're so beautiful. Cardinals have always been my favorite bird." Hannah gazed at the burst of crimson filling the branch.

Cody nodded. "Looks like a Christmas card. These woods are a bird-watcher's paradise."

"Hurry up!" McKenzie called from the top of the hill.

Cody and Hannah continued their climb. They joined the twins and the dogs at the top.

"Since I beat Madison up here, I get to pick my tree first." McKenzie ran to Cody's side.

"Okay, but let's take our time," Cody instructed.

McKenzie and Madison followed Cody's advice and walked slowly along the path, touching the branches of variously sized trees and chattering among themselves.

"This might sound like a silly question, but how will we get two trees back down the hill and to your house?" Hannah looked down at the sloping trail. "It seems to me we need a little more manpower than you, me and two six-year-olds. Will we need to make two trips?"

Cody smiled. "Do you think I'd make you trudge up the mountainside twice in one day?"

Hannah scanned her surroundings. "I think I could do it."

"I have no doubt you could, but there's a better way. We'll cut the trees and then hike back to my brother Jake's house. He and Olivia plan to take the kids ice-skating at Fletcher's Pond later this afternoon. You and I can jump on my all-terrain four-wheeler and head back up for the trees."

Hannah hesitated for a second and looked up at the sky. Cody wasn't sure if she was contemplating the ride alone with him or the weather conditions. "My offer to drive you home if the roads are bad still stands, so there's no need to worry."

She smiled before answering. "The four-wheeler sounds like fun."

Cody exhaled a breath he hadn't realized he was holding. Maybe he'd get that walk alone in the woods with Hannah after all.

"Uncle Cody! I found my tree," McKenzie yelled, pulling him from thoughts of a potential romantic walk.

"Let's go check it out. Knowing McKenzie, she's picked out the biggest tree on the mountain," Cody laughed. He rested his hand on her lower back to guide her in the direction of the twins. Their boots crunched in the snow and the flakes continued to fall.

"This is such a wonderful thing you're doing for the girls. They'll carry these memories with them for the rest of their lives."

"I hope so." Cody appreciated Hannah's encouraging words. The twins deserved to experience special moments like today. Perhaps he could provide them with a future filled with love and even greater experiences.

Cody and Hannah caught up to the girls.

"This is it." McKenzie pointed to a smaller, sparse tree.

Cody had to admit he was surprised by McKenzie's choice. With an abundance of gorgeous and full trees, why would she pick one that looked like it might not even live until Christmas Day? "Are you sure that's the one?" He pointed to another beside it. A tree that appeared much healthier and robust.

McKenzie shook her head with authority. "Nope. I want this one." She fingered its delicate branches, causing a few needles to fall on the snow-covered ground.

Madison moved closer to her sister, crinkling her nose. "It doesn't look too good."

The sound of snow mixing with intermittent light rain filled the surrounding woods.

McKenzie continued to study her selection. "That's why I

want it. If I don't take it home, no one will pick it and it might die before it ever has a chance to become a real Christmas tree with decorations and everything. Please, Uncle Cody. Can I have this one?"

For a second, Cody wondered if McKenzie felt like the distressed tree. Did she fear she and Madison would be left alone if he didn't man up and keep his word to his best friend by filing for adoption? He rested his hand on her shoulder. "I think you've made an excellent choice."

McKenzie looked up with a smile that melted his heart.

"It might be okay, if we give it lots of water," Madison reassured her sister.

Hannah stepped closer. "Have you decided on your tree, Madison?"

"Yes!" Madison ran over to a nearby pine tree, grabbing hold of its branch and shaking off the snow. "This is the one I want."

Cody placed his bag on the ground and opened the zipper. "I think you both made excellent choices. Are you ready to cut them down?" He removed a junior-sized handsaw that he'd shown to the girls earlier this morning.

The twins jumped up and down. "We're ready!"

Cody turned to Hannah. "Would you like to help McKenzie first? After, you can take care of Madison's tree."

"Yes, please Miss Simpson," McKenzie pleaded while Cody handed off the handsaw.

"Are you sure? I've never done this before."

McKenzie took Hannah's hand. "It's okay. I can show you how to do it. It's easy."

Cody winked at Hannah. "You'll do fine."

Hannah and McKenzie worked together with the saw. With little effort, since the trunk wasn't thick, the tree toppled over.

The twins cheered. Cody watched Hannah as her eyes lit up with joy, but then he thought he noticed a glint of sadness.

"Are you crying, Miss Simpson?" Madison asked.

Cody hadn't imagined it. He moved closer, taking notice of the moisture around her eyelashes. He gently placed his hand underneath her chin and tipped it upward. "Hey, are you okay?"

Hannah quickly looked away and wiped her eyes. "Yes, I'm fine—just a little embarrassed. The holidays always make me sentimental."

"Christmas should make you happy. It's when Jesus was born!" Madison swung her arms open.

Hannah laughed and looked down to Madison. "You're right, sweetie. It is the time to celebrate and be joyful. So how about we cut your tree down now?"

Cody wondered if maybe Hannah wanted a tree of her own. "The four-wheeler vehicle is big enough for you to pick out a tree, if you'd like. But I think we might need to hurry. I can feel the temperature rising, which isn't conducive for snow."

Hannah turned away from him. "Thank you for the offer, but I hadn't planned on getting a tree this year."

No tree? Cody was confused and full of questions. Why wouldn't Hannah want to put up a tree? She appeared to love everything that went along with celebrating the holiday season. It seemed odd that she wouldn't want to have a Christmas tree of her own. Something wasn't adding up. As he considered her earlier tearful breakdown, the snow turned into rain.

Early Friday evening, Hannah finalized the note to leave at Garrison's Mercantile for the Matthews family. Like before, she'd drop it off before the store opened. In secret, she'd been able to leave cash to cover two grocery deliveries from Garrison's Mercantile without Nellie figuring out who was making the donations. A miraculous accomplishment, considering Nellie's all-knowing ways.

In addition to providing groceries, Hannah had purchased a

fresh-cut tree and had it delivered to the Matthews' house yesterday. She'd also finalized organizing the fireworks display. Everything was on track for a successful Christmas festival.

The kettle on the stove whistled. She pushed away from the paperwork at the kitchen table to pour herself a hot cup of cinnamon stick tea. Memories of Christmas past filled her head as the steam rose into her face while she bobbed the tea bag up and down in her favorite holiday mug.

Hannah reclaimed her seat at the table and gazed outside the bay window. Once darkness fell, the timer Mr. O'Brien placed on the outdoor lights would turn on, signaling to the outside world she was excited and ready for Christmas. But that was all a front to conceal the pain in her heart. As Christmas neared, along with the painful anniversary of losing her family, the more difficult it was becoming to keep her past a secret.

Over the past several days, Hannah struggled with anxiety teetering on a full-blown panic attack. Fortunately, the most recent attack occurred within the confines of her home, away from anyone who would be full of questions. All it took to trigger that episode was her daughter's favorite Christmas song playing on the radio. Had she been kidding herself to believe planning the festival would help her through the difficult holiday season? So far that hadn't been the case.

Headlights flashed, filling the kitchen at the same time Hannah heard the sound of a diesel engine pulling into her driveway. She wasn't expecting company. The Friday night plan was to put on her cozy flannel pajamas, have popcorn for her dinner and watch Hallmark movies. With plans to meet Cody and the lighting crew at the town square first thing in the morning, she wanted to get to bed early.

She peeked through the window.

Cody's truck. What was he doing here?

Hannah shot to the table and scrambled to clear away the

paperwork. The incriminating evidence that proved she's the town's Secret Santa. Rumors had been swirling around town the past week. No one had solved the mystery and Hannah wanted to keep it that way. The cost of the fireworks show alone was enough to make people question how a teacher could afford these Christmas surprises on her salary. Revealing her identity could expose the fact that Hannah's husband had been well insured, making her a multimillionaire. Of course, she would trade every last penny to have her family back.

The doorbell rang just as Hannah shoved the receipts for the new computers she'd purchased for the town library into the utensil drawer. She released a breath, smoothed her hair and headed to the door to invite her guest inside.

"Ho ho ho!" Cody exclaimed when Hannah pulled open the front door.

Startled by seeing Cody dressed in a Santa suit and holding his belly, Hannah was speechless before she broke into laughter. "What in the world?"

"Good, you're home." He raced down the three steps and headed back to his truck. The white beard strapped to his chin waved in the breeze. Upon his return, he pulled a tree up the steps. A tree much larger than what she'd helped the twins cut down last weekend.

Hannah covered her mouth both in surprise and to conceal her laughter. He made an adorable Santa. Correction. He made a gorgeous Santa.

"I know last weekend you said you didn't want a tree, but it's Christmas. What's Christmas without a tree? The minute I saw this one, I knew it was meant for you. If this is too big, I've got one that's a little smaller on my truck. I planned to take it to the Matthews' place, but Nellie told me they had a tree delivered by an anonymous donor last night. Apparently, someone has been sending them food also. I thought it was

Nellie, but she swears it's not her, but I think she's determined to find out the identity of the town's Secret Santa."

Hannah hoped she'd covered her tracks well enough that Nellie wouldn't follow it back to her. She pulled the door open wider and stepped aside. "It's gorgeous. Please, bring it on inside." Not only had he brought a tree, he'd even thought to bring a stand along with a tree skirt.

Cody's broad smile caused one side of his beard to pull loose. He carried the tree into the foyer. "Should I put it in the family room?"

When Hannah first moved into the house, she imagined having a tree in the same room as the fireplace so she could snuggle by the fire and enjoy the twinkling lights. But the closer it got to the holiday, the thought of celebrating alone was too painful. "Yes, to the right of the fireplace would be perfect."

Cody followed Hannah's instructions. First, he spread out the skirt and placed the tree inside of the stand. Next, he tightened the brackets to keep it sturdy. "Do you have ornaments? If you don't, I brought some. They're out in my truck."

Did Cody want to stay and help her decorate the tree? Should she extend an invitation or just thank him for the kind gesture and let him go home. A part of her wasn't ready for him to leave. No. Not a good idea. He probably didn't even want to stay.

"I can help you put up the decorations. The tree is tall. I wouldn't want you getting up on a ladder while you're alone in the house."

Excitement bubbled. He didn't want to leave. How could she say no to his offer? Cody had gone out of his way to cut down the perfect tree for her and to dress up as Santa. But using her own ornaments wasn't an option. Not with Cody present. Hannah couldn't bring herself to release all of the memories packed away. Homemade ornaments her daughter made using

Popsicle sticks. The *Our First Christmas* bulb given to her by her husband after they'd moved into the tiny one-bedroom apartment in Phoenix. She couldn't forget her favorite ornament of all…*Baby's First Christmas*. Rick brought it home the day after they'd found out she was pregnant with Jenna, even though it had been the middle of July.

"Maybe it would be best if we used your ornaments. Mine are all packed away in the basement somewhere. It's a mess down there. It could take all night to find them." Hannah didn't like to be dishonest with Cody. The truth was, she knew exactly what was inside of each box. Opening them in front of him would be too risky. Tightness squeezed the inside of her chest.

"You got it. I'll run out to my truck and bring them in." Cody pulled off his Santa hat and flung it on the foyer table, along with the beard. "Maybe you can turn on a little Christmas music?" he suggested before heading out the door.

Hannah stood frozen for a moment, considering how her quiet evening alone had made a complete one-eighty from earlier. She caught a glimpse of herself in the mirror over the table. "Oh my!" The unruly cowlick that she has fought since she was a child stood at attention.

A quick peek outside the window told her she had a minute to at least run a comb through her hair, or maybe a ponytail was necessary. Hannah sprinted down the hallway to her bedroom and headed in the bathroom. Grabbing for a brush and hair clip, she quickly tackled the cowlick, along with the unmanageable locks and captured it into a messy bun. Better. But upon further inspection under the light, her face looked pale. She opened the vanity drawer, removed a tube of tinted gloss, and swiped it across her lips once and then again.

Outside, the sound of Cody slamming the door to his truck told Hannah he was on his way back inside the house. *This is as good as it gets.* She rolled her eyes at her reflection. *Now—if you can just remember to breathe.*

Hannah made it back to the family room seconds before Cody returned. His woodsy scent filled the room as he moved closer.

"I have another box outside if you'd like to decorate the mantel or anything else." He placed the large container on the hardwood.

Hannah took a seat on the floor. "I think these will be enough for now. You really are Santa Claus."

Cody sat across from Hannah and opened the box. "Sometimes I get a little carried away when it comes to Christmas. I think I inherited it from my mother. It was her favorite holiday."

"Is she still with you?" Hannah had met all of Cody's brothers except the youngest, Luke.

"She and my father live in Denver. My mother has Alzheimer's, so she's in a nursing home since we were no longer able to provide the care she needed. My father is with her every day."

"I'm sorry. It's a terrible disease. Your mother is blessed to have your father looking after her."

Cody nodded. "He's always been a loving husband. For as long as I can remember, he's treated my mother like they were just married. I can only hope to be as good of a husband one day."

"Have you ever been close?" Hannah was surprised by her own question.

Cody's hand froze for a second as he removed a shiny ornament from the box. "Up until four months ago, I thought my future was set in stone."

Hannah knew all too well that no one knows what the future holds. At one time, she had had a loving husband and a beautiful daughter. It was the life she'd always dreamed of having. And then everything changed. She was well aware how difficult it could be to talk about events from the past. "I'm sorry. I shouldn't have asked that question. This is meant to be a festive time. You don't have to say any more."

"No, it's all right. My brothers keep reminding me how important it is to talk about painful events rather than keep them bottled up inside." Cody rolled the bulb in his hands. "Can I be honest with you about something?"

"Of course." Hannah bit her lower lip.

"Since we've been spending more time together. I haven't really thought much about Mallory—she was my fiancée. We met years ago, while I was competing as a professional bull rider. We dated here and there for a while before I retired. After I left competition, I wanted to settle down, but she wasn't ready so we broke up. Over a year ago, we reconnected. She said she'd changed her mind and was ready for a commitment." Cody shook his head. "I should have known better, but we started seeing each other again and she accepted my proposal. I thought maybe things were different, but once McKenzie and Madison came to live with me things between us changed. A month later she ran off with a much younger rodeo superstar."

Hannah remained silent. She sensed Cody wasn't finished.

"The twins thought it was their fault that Mallory didn't like them. I knew that wasn't the reason. She wasn't ready to settle down. The thrill of being a part of the rodeo circuit was something she could never give up. I knew that after I retired and we broke up the first time. Trying to make things work the second time with her was bad judgment on my part."

"That doesn't make the pain any easier."

"No, but I only recently realized that being a bull rider was what I did, not who I was. Mallory was only interested in that part of me." Cody straightened his shoulders.

"Thank you for sharing that with me." She reached out and placed her hand over Cody's. "I know it's not always easy to talk about the past."

"You make it easy." Cody fixed his gaze on her. "You've made a lot of things easier for me, not just with the festival, but you've helped me to realize maybe I can be a good father to the girls."

A moment of silence filled the room.

"I guess we better get to work on the tree." Hannah stood and moved toward the television. She set the channel to sounds of the season.

"That's a perfect choice." Cody stood and hung the first ornament on the tree.

Hannah took a deep breath to take control of her increasing heart rate. Until this evening, Hannah knew little about Cody's personal life, outside of caring for the twins. Since their initial meeting, she had every intention of keeping her focus on planning the Christmas festival and not on Cody. But now, as he stood next to the Christmas tree he'd cut down and brought to her home, looking completely adorable in the Santa suit, she had to admit the truth. She was falling for Cody Beckett.

Chapter Eleven

The day before the start of the Christmas festival, Cody arrived at Garrison's Mercantile. He was running around like a headless chicken, trying to tie up any loose ends, but it felt like a losing battle.

Earlier in the week, the mayor had called him and Hannah to his office with good news. A large unexpected monetary donation had been made to the festival, which left Cody and Hannah scrambling to reinstate some of their previously canceled plans due to the budget shortfall.

"I was just getting ready to call you," Nellie called out from across the store when Cody stepped inside the door and removed his Stetson.

"What's up?" Cody had a short list of items to pick up at the market before he picked up the girls from school. Today was their last day before Christmas break, so no doubt their excitement levels would be through the roof this afternoon.

"Hank picked up the extra tables for the vendors. He'll have them set up for you before the festival kicks off tomorrow evening. Can you believe the big day is upon us?" Nellie carried a plate of warm brownies and placed them on the counter where Cody stood.

Planning for the festival had been a challenge, but Cody wouldn't have traded one moment of the time it had allowed him to spend with Hannah and to give the twins a special

Christmas. "It did sneak up on us." He picked up the baked good and smiled. "This is just the pick-me-up I need. Thanks!" Cody took a bite, savoring the fudgy treat. "Man, these are so good."

Nellie laughed. "I baked at least fifteen dozen."

"I've got first dibs on any that you don't sell." Cody popped the last bite into his mouth before grabbing another. "The girls are going to be keyed up this afternoon. I need to make sure my energy level stays up. They've been bouncing off the walls with excitement."

"Christmas is a magical time for children." Nellie clutched her hands together and smiled. "Everyone is excited for the start of the festival. Have you been by the town square today?" Nellie grabbed the coffee pot of fresh brew from behind the counter and poured Cody a cup. "The lighting crew has been working since early this morning on both the tree and the surrounding lights. I can't wait for the lighting ceremony tomorrow night."

"Thanks." Cody took a sip of the coffee. The extra money recently donated had allowed Hannah and Cody to go all out with a tree bigger than any the town had displayed in years past. "I haven't had a chance to get over there. Logan and I had to make a trip up to Denver to meet with a potential handler and his family."

"So you haven't seen the fountain?" Nellie's eyes widened.

"No, what's up with it?"

"Oh, I guess maybe I should have kept my mouth shut. Hannah never said it was a surprise though."

Cody scratched the top of his head. "It's too late now." He glanced at his watch. "I've got time before picking up the girls. I can go over there myself."

Nellie blew out a breath. "Okay, but don't tell Hannah I said anything. Make sure you act surprised when you see it."

Cody crossed his heart. His curiosity was getting the best of him. "I promise. So spill it already. I know you're dying to tell me anyway," he said, smiling.

"This morning, while I was taking my daily walk, I went through the town square to check things out. Over the past week, each time I've walked that path there's been something new to see. It's been exciting to watch the transformation. Today, I saw Hannah there with three men at the fountain. Of course, I couldn't resist asking what was happening."

When Nellie stopped talking, Cody assumed someone had entered the store. He looked around even though he hadn't heard the front door bell. "And?"

Nellie's smile lit up her face. "They're putting together an outdoor ice rink around the fountain. Isn't that exciting? Everyone will love it!"

Earlier in their planning, Cody and Hannah had crunched the numbers on the cost of having an outdoor ice rink. Even with the generous donations, Cody didn't think there was enough money left over to cover the expense, so they decided to cut it from their list. "Are you sure that's what was happening?"

Nellie nodded. "Hannah said a second donation had come in for the festival, so there was plenty of money left. According to her, there's enough funds to arrange for the fireworks display on the closing night."

Cody scratched the side of his head. Was that what the mayor had called about? Earlier in the day, while he and Logan were in Denver for their meeting, he'd sent a call from the mayor to his voicemail. Once they'd finished up, he and Logan were busy chatting about how well things went during their meeting. He'd completely forgotten to check his messages. Another anonymous donation? This was indeed an unexpected surprise. "Any idea who it could be?" The all-knowing Nellie had to have some idea.

"I'm still investigating." She winked. "I can't help but think the monetary donations are from the same person who's helping the Matthews family."

Cody wondered what kind of investigative work Nellie was conducting. He remembered how Nellie had told him she'd seen Hannah at the store in the early morning hours when the first grocery donation was made to the family. "What makes you think that?"

Nellie shrugged her shoulder and smiled.

Were all of the donations coming from the same person? Was Hannah the town's Secret Santa? Cody's mind was reeling. "Well, whoever is responsible, it's great news." Cody eyed the brownies, tempted to eat a third, but decided to display some willpower.

"Hannah was thrilled. She went on and on about how pleased you would be." Nellie looked around the store and leaned in a little closer. "I probably shouldn't tell you this, but since you're like the son I never had, I will. It's been obvious to me that Hannah is quite smitten with you. Do you plan to ask her to the Christmas dance?" Her eyes sparkled.

Cody forced down the lump that lodged in his throat. Was Nellie right? She usually knew all. Is Hannah really interested in him? He'd never thought about asking her to the dance. They'd both be there of course since they're in charge…but a date?

"You better hurry up. Yesterday in the store I overheard Caleb Swanson talking on his phone. I don't know who he was talking to, but he mentioned asking Hannah to the dance."

Caleb Swanson?

Cody's stomach twisted like a pretzel. They didn't have anything in common. Was Hannah interested in him? Had they been on a date already? She'd never mentioned anything to him, but then again, why would she? So far, Hannah kept her private life tighter than a new jar of peanut butter.

"Dear, your face looks like a cherry tomato. Are you okay?" Nellie rested her hand on Cody's arm.

It was time to come clean. For a second time, Cody glanced

around the store. "Okay, what I'm going to tell you can't go beyond these walls. Can you make that promise to me?"

"Of course. I might know a lot of things that go on in this town, but there's one thing I don't do. I don't spread gossip. If someone tells me something in confidence it stays here." Nellie lifted her hands and motioned like she was zipping her lips.

Cody had to talk with someone. He could trust Nellie with his secret. Like she said, he was the son she'd never had. "First, I need to know if Caleb and Hannah have actually gone out on a legitimate date." He held his breath and waited for an answer.

"No, not yet. After Caleb ended his call, he asked me if I knew anything about Hannah's personal life. He questioned whether or not she was dating anyone."

Cody's brow arched. "Wait, before we go any further, isn't this spreading gossip? I don't want to put you in an uncomfortable position."

"Absolutely not. Caleb never asked me to keep any part of our conversation quiet. In fact, he specifically asked if I would talk to Hannah for him." Nellie kept a firm chin.

What? Was Caleb in junior high? The guy didn't even have the guts to ask Hannah to the dance himself? Instead, he needed the sweet, elderly store owner to ask on his behalf. Cody's first instincts were correct. There was no way Caleb was Hannah's type of guy. So what was he going to do about it?

First, he needed to know why Nellie had the impression that Hannah was interested in him. Sure, there were times when they were together planning for the festival that he caught her stealing looks at him. Then, there was last Friday when he brought the tree to her house. Cody sensed a vibe from Hannah, like maybe she was attracted to him. Or was that only wishful thinking on his part?

"Have you talked to Hannah about Caleb?"

Nellie shook her head. "No. I wanted to let you know his intentions first."

"Earlier you mentioned Hannah was smitten with me. What makes you say that?"

"Trust me." Nellie placed her hand on Cody's arm. "Working in the store all of these years has taught me how to read people. There's no doubt in my mind that Hannah has developed feelings for you, but for whatever reason, I believe she's fighting them."

Cody could relate. There was nothing more he'd rather do than brush aside his fear of getting involved in another relationship. So why didn't he? If not now, when? One thing he knew for sure was that he wanted a family. Was he going to stand by and allow Caleb to worm his way into Hannah's life?

The bell over the front door jingled, breaking the hush that hung in the air.

Cody turned, not recognizing the young couple who'd stepped inside.

"Welcome to Garrison's. Please let me know if I can help you find anything." Nellie waved to the couple.

"Let me grab what I need and I'll get out of your hair. I know you like to make new customers feel like part of the town." Cody rested his hand on Nellie's arm. "Thanks for talking with me. I can't discuss affairs of the heart any longer with my mother. I'm blessed to have you as my second mom."

Nellie brushed away a tear trickling down her cheek. "Dear, from the moment I saw you and Hannah together for the first time, I knew there was a spark that couldn't be ignored. And why would you want to? Life is so much sweeter when you share it with someone you love. I don't want you to miss out on that."

Cody stepped toward Nellie and gave her a hug.

Several minutes later, Cody walked out of the store while Nellie fed the out-of-town couple her homemade brownies. He placed the bag of groceries on the floor of the passenger seat and headed toward the school to pick up the girls. Nellie was right. Sharing your life with someone you love was what mattered the most. Asking Hannah to the dance would be a big step, but one he was ready to take. He only hoped that Caleb didn't beat him to the punch.

"Everything looks perfect and so festive." Nellie flashed a joyful smile.

Hannah gazed around the town square. A group of carolers strolled down the sidewalk singing and passing out candy canes to the children.

"Look how many people are already here, and the tree lighting isn't for another two hours," Nellie noted.

Friday evening had finally arrived and the big event was about to start. Hannah was pleased so far with the turnout. She only hoped one of those many people milling about didn't turn out to be the unexpected visitor she'd had earlier in the day.

Hannah had been buzzing around her house, attending to several last-minute details on her list when her doorbell rang. She hoped it was her neighbor, Mr. O'Brien, since she had a plate of freshly baked cookies for him. When she'd opened the front door, she quickly learned it wasn't her neighbor. To her surprise, it was Caleb Swanson holding a handful of flowers along with a huge goofy grin. When she immediately started to sneeze, she didn't have the heart to tell him she was allergic to daisies. Instead, she told him she thought she was coming down with a cold. What surprised Hannah even more was Caleb's invitation to the Christmas dance on the last night of the festival.

Hannah turned to Nellie. "There's plenty of activities to keep everyone entertained until we light the tree," Hannah explained.

"Have you seen Cody today?" Nellie asked with a mischievous grin.

"No. He texted me this morning. He had to run up to Denver to deliver something to his father, but he wanted to make sure I brought my ice skates tonight." Hannah watched Nellie's reaction before she glanced at her watch. "He should be here any minute. He mentioned you told him about the ice rink."

Nellie fiddled with her white angora scarf. "I hope you're not upset. After you mentioned the additional donation and your brilliant idea to turn the fountain and the surrounding area into a rink, I couldn't keep the exciting news to myself." Nellie leaned in a little closer and fixated her eyes on Hannah. "Any idea on who this mystery Secret Santa is? I have someone in mind, but I haven't confirmed it."

Hannah wasn't sure if she was being paranoid, but something in Nellie's eyes and tone made her wonder if she had cracked the case. Had Nellie seen her creep up the steps of the store in the early morning hours to leave the envelope of cash for the Matthews family? Was it possible the store had cameras out front? "No, I don't have any idea."

Did Nellie have her as the prime suspect in her mystery? Hannah needed to send her into another direction. "Now that I think about it," Hannah said, placing her hand under her chin. She might as well play it up. "A couple of days ago while Cody and I were doing some brainstorming at the pavilion, we saw Nelson Whitfield at the fountain. There was a man I didn't recognize with Nelson. They looked like they were measuring the area around the fountain." Hannah sent up a silent prayer asking for forgiveness for the little white lie she was telling, that it was for a good cause. At least that's what she told herself. If anyone were to discover she was the town's Secret Santa, it would get back to Cody. Then he'd not only find out she once had a family, but she was also worth a lot of money. Hannah needed to be the one to tell Cody—she just didn't know how.

"I can't imagine Nelson would have that kind of money. He's worked as a plumber all of his life. Besides, he just had to put a new roof on his house and barn. He went on and on about the expense." Nellie shook her head.

"I'm just telling you what I saw. Maybe he and his wife are good savers." Hannah had no idea about Nelson's saving habits, but she was desperate. Nellie was smart and had ways of finding things out that no one could explain.

"Maybe, but I think it's someone else." Nellie turned. "Look who's coming."

From across the town square, Hannah watched the twins run toward the pavilion.

"Miss Simpson! We're so happy you're here." Madison and McKenzie looked like two little snow bunnies, bundled up in their matching white puffer coats and knit caps. Each had a red scarf tied around their necks. Hannah had to admit Cody had a sense of fashion when it came to dressing the twins.

"Hello girls. It's good to see you."

"Uncle Cody is coming. He bought us ice skates today so we can all go skating after the tree lighting," Madison explained.

"But first we're going to have hot chocolate after the lights. I want to try the peppermint." McKenzie jumped up and down.

"What about one of my peppermint brownies?" Nellie suggested. "I've tried a new recipe and I thought you two could be my guinea pigs."

The twins giggled.

"Sure we can. I've never had that either," McKenzie said, cheering.

Cody approached, dressed in jeans and a black coat. Hannah couldn't pull her eyes away. Wearing his Stetson, he looked like a handsome cowboy one would see at the rodeo.

"Hello ladies." Cody stopped beside Nellie, holding tight to Hershey's leash.

Hannah moved to the animal, bent down and rubbed her face into the dog's coat. "I'm so happy you brought Hershey."

"Well, since the festival is dog-friendly, I thought she'd enjoy the outing."

McKenzie looked up at Hannah. "I wanted to bring Ellie too since you love her so much."

"Yeah, Uncle Cody said you'd be too busy. Maybe you can come over tomorrow and visit her?" Madison suggested.

"Tomorrow is the big snowman-making contest. Miss Simpson and I will be busy judging," Cody said.

Nellie smiled. "That's right, and you two will be participating in the contest. Do you plan to build one together or separately?"

McKenzie looked at Madison. "We're going to build it together, right?"

Her sister nodded. "Yeah, McKenzie is better with the head and face than I am. I'll do the middle part."

"She means his big stomach. Madison is good at that."

Hannah's heart warmed at the twins. She loved how they complimented each other and enjoyed being together.

Nellie addressed Cody. "I can take Hershey if you and Hannah need to get ready for the lighting. The girls can come with me. Hank is setting up the tables in front of the store."

"Yay! Can we?" McKenzie cheered. "I want to try a peppermint brownie."

"Okay." Cody looked at his watch. "Make sure you head back to the pavilion by seven o'clock. I wouldn't want either one of you to miss the lighting."

"We won't. I want to see the carolers sing 'Rudolph, the Red-Nosed Reindeer,'" Madison giggled.

Nellie and the twins headed to the store with Hershey leading the way.

"Can I buy you a hot chocolate?" Cody offered.

Hannah tightened her scarf. "That sounds wonderful. It does feel colder tonight."

Cody's shoulder brushed against Hannah while they strolled

to the vendors selling treats and beverages. "I checked the weather before leaving the house. There's snow in the forecast," Cody reported.

The aromas of funnel cakes and sweet cinnamon filled the air.

"Two hot chocolates with extra whipped cream, Mary Ann." Cody placed the order and pulled his wallet from his pocket.

"No, these are on the house." Mary Ann waved her hand. "After all of the work the two of you have done getting the festival ready, I can't take your money."

"Thank you. But at least you can take a tip."

Hannah watched as Cody wrapped a one-dollar bill around a twenty. "Smooth move," she said as they stepped out of line with their beverages in hand.

"They've worked hard too. They should be compensated." Cody took a drink, leaving a dollop of whipped cream on his lip.

Hannah laughed and covered her mouth with her gloved hand.

"What's so funny?"

"You have some whipped cream stuck to your lip."

Cody smiled and wiped it away. "Thanks. So tell me, did the mayor have any idea about that second donation? I was in a meeting when he called about it. Needless to say, it was a big surprise when I heard we had funds for the ice rink."

"I hope you were okay with me making arrangements on my own. I know we talked earlier about making decisions together."

Cody shook his head. "Oh no. You did the right thing. We were under a time crunch. I'm happy that you took the reins."

"I'm glad you're okay with it. Actually, the mayor didn't know where the money came from. I suppose that doesn't really matter. The important thing is we've been able to put together a festival that hopefully the town will remember for years to come."

"Still, I'd like to know, wouldn't you?" Cody eyed Hannah.

That feeling she got from Nellie earlier returned. Was Cody suspicious of Hannah too? She wasn't going to use the Nelson fib again. One untruth was enough for the day. "Well, I guess you never know if the donor will reveal their identity once the holidays are over. For now, let's just be thankful."

Cody nodded. "You're right."

They continued to walk down the sidewalk. The festive lights sparkled as the first snowflakes began to fall.

"This is perfect. We couldn't ask for better weather for the start of the festivities." Hannah took a deep breath and snuck a peek at Cody. Her heartbeat pounded inside her chest.

"Are you ready for the dance? I mean, do you have a date or anything?"

Hannah's stomach squeezed when she thought of poor Caleb. After she told him she had to work at the dance and wouldn't be able to go with him, he'd looked like a sad little puppy. It was the right thing to do. She didn't want to lead him on. There was only one person she was interested in going to the dance with and he was standing in front of her. "Well, I... funny you should ask."

Cody's eyes widened. "What does that mean? Did Caleb beat me to the punch?"

Wait. How did he know about Caleb? "What made you ask that? Are you friends with him?"

"No. I mean, I know who he is, but we're not friends. Yesterday, Nellie mentioned he planned to ask you to the dance."

"How did she know?"

Cody laughed. "He was questioning Nellie about your relationship situation...if you were dating anyone."

Only in a small town. Hannah had hoped to keep the incident with Caleb between the two of them.

"So, did he ask you?"

"Actually, he showed up at my house this morning, carrying a handful of daisies."

"That's nice."

"It would have been if I wasn't highly allergic to that flower. Since I was a little girl, whenever I come close to daisies, I either break out in a rash or start to sneeze uncontrollably," Hannah explained.

"Oh man. Now I feel sorry for the guy. Well, only if you said no." Cody gave a sly grin.

Hannah's pulse ticked up. She felt like a teenage girl. "I said no."

"Have you gone on a date with him?"

"No. I was completely caught off guard by his visit to my house."

"My guess is that Caleb was more surprised by your reaction to the daisies," Cody chuckled.

Hannah did feel terrible. "I told Caleb I had to work at the dance so being a participant wasn't an option."

"Actually, by the time the dance starts our work will be done. There really won't be anything either of us will have to do in regard to preparation. We can relax and know that we've done our job," Cody said reasonably.

Hannah nodded. "I guess you're right. But the truth is there's only one person I'd like to have as my date and it isn't Caleb."

Cody stepped closer.

Hannah's insides vibrated when he took her hand. His warm breath tickled her cheek.

"Will you be my date to the dance?"

Adrenaline shot through Hannah's body. It was Cody, not Caleb. She relaxed and sighed happily. "There's nothing more I'd rather do."

Chapter Twelve

Cody glanced at the kitchen clock and frowned. As usual, they were running late. "Hurry up and eat your cereal, girls. You still have to get dressed and get your teeth brushed."

Giggles and whispers filled the warm space. Cody had turned on the fireplace earlier to take away the chill.

"What's so funny?" He eyed the twins huddled together exchanging whispers.

"Nothing, we're just eating." McKenzie looked up from her bowl.

"Since it's snowing, are we going to pick up Miss Simpson and drive her to the festival?" Madison asked before McKenzie let out another giggle.

Cody had a feeling the twins' silly behavior was because of their teacher. They were still plotting ways to start a romance between him and Hannah. Last night, before tucking them into bed, he'd overheard them talking about the Christmas dance. They were scheming ways to make sure their uncle and their teacher attended the dance together. Little did they know he'd already made sure that would happen. Cody had decided to keep that to himself for now.

"I hadn't thought about it, but it might be a good idea. Miss Simpson doesn't like to drive on snowy roads," Cody said, thinking out loud.

"Yay! I heard the weatherman on TV say it's going to snow

all day. By the time the festival is over it might be ten feet deep!" Madison announced.

"It doesn't snow that much." McKenzie rolled her eyes at her twin before turning her attention back to her cereal.

"No, but you're right. It might be nasty later. Maybe I better text Miss Simpson and at least offer her a ride." If he could spend extra time with Hannah, he was all for it.

Again, the whispers started.

Cody picked up his phone and typed a quick text.

The weather could be bad later. Would you like for us to pick you up?

A few moments passed before the tiny dots appeared on the phone. Cody's heart beat against his chest.

That sounds great. What time?

I need to stop by Garrison's before heading to the festival. Do you want me to pick you up after?

Actually, I need to go by there myself. We can go together, if you'd like.

Great. We'll be over within the hour. The twins are moving a little slow this morning.

I'll be ready.

Cody placed his phone on the counter and smiled. Once the festival came to an end, he wouldn't have a reason to see Hannah as often. Unless she wanted to volunteer more time helping with the dogs, he might only see her on a weekend here or there. The thought made him feel like the deflated blow-up Santa he saw outside of Mr. Pepperoni the other morning.

"Did she say yes?" McKenzie asked.

"She did. I told her we'd come and pick her up within an hour, so you better get moving."

Both girls cheered and for the third time since sitting down to breakfast they started a whispered conversation.

"Okay, spill it. What are the two of you up to?"

"We think you should ask Miss Simpson to be your date at the Christmas dance," Madison said.

"Yeah, why don't you ask her, Uncle Cody? I heard Mr. Caleb wants to take Miss Simpson to the dance," McKenzie added.

The way news spread around this town was mind-boggling. "Where did you hear that?"

"Lisa, from our class, said her mom talked to Miss Nellie. I think Miss Simpson likes you, not Mr. Caleb. You should hurry up and ask her. You don't want to go alone," Madison explained, sounding much older than her age.

"I won't be alone if I'm with you and your sister. I thought you guys were going to be my dates," Cody joked with the twins.

"Dances aren't really for kids. It's more for grown-ups. We'll have snacks and stuff to eat. Plus, we'll be hanging out with our friends," Madison continued.

Time was running short. Cody decided he'd play with the girls a little while longer and keep them wondering about the dance. "You need to finish up your breakfasts. We don't want to be late for the snowman-making contest."

"They can't start without you and Miss Simpson. You guys are the judges!" McKenzie picked up her bowl of cereal and drank the remaining milk.

Later that morning Cody, Hannah and the girls arrived at the town square following a quick stop at Garrison's Mercantile. Upon their arrival at the store, Nellie had raced to the door to greet them. Overwhelmed with excitement, she could hardly speak. According to her, the mayor had stopped by with the news of two additional anonymous donations. The first was an undisclosed sum gifted to the Matthews family. Mayor Jennings told Nellie it was enough to cover the outstanding balance owed for Joe's knee surgery and the current amount due for Joyce's treatment. Nellie was forced to slow down and take a breath before sharing that an additional $10,000 was deposited into the account for the children's toy drive. The mayor had quickly notified the committee from church, who had already begun shopping for gifts to be presented the last day of the festival.

While Nellie continued to go on about the blessings bestowed on the town, Cody had kept a close eye on Hannah. She'd remained unusually quiet, but then again, she hadn't been her normal talkative self since he and the twins had picked her up. But there was something about her response to Nellie's news that once again made him question whether or not she had played a part in these generous gifts.

"The contest is going to start soon. Would you like for me to grab us some hot chocolate?" Hannah offered, breaking into Cody's suspicions.

"You read my mind. I planned on sending the girls, but they were so excited to see the ice rink with Jake and his family, I never had a chance to ask."

"Not a problem. I'll run over and pick up the drinks." Hannah spoke in a tone devoid of emotion. She turned and headed to the hot chocolate kiosk with her head down.

Cody watched Hannah walk away. This wasn't the Hannah he knew. She normally carried her head high and walked with an upbeat pace. Something was on her mind. Perhaps after the contest he could get her to open up to him.

He busied himself with arranging the sign-up sheet on the

table and making some changes to the digital copy on his tablet.

"Do you have a second, Cody?"

Cody looked up from the task at hand. "Sure, Nellie. What's up?"

Nellie looked around and stepped forward, closing the distance between the two. "I think I've solved the mystery."

It was best to play dumb. "What are you referring to?" Cody stifled a grin.

She playfully slapped his arm. "Come on. We don't have time for games. You know what I'm talking about. All of the mysterious donations…the town's Secret Santa."

Cody laughed. "Oh yeah, right. Okay, who is it?"

Nellie reached into her purse and fished out a couple pieces of folded paper. "Take a look at these." She unfolded each page and lined them up side by side along the table.

"What are they?" Cody needed to invest in a pair of reading glasses.

"These are the instructions that were left on the doorstep of the store for the money donated to the Matthews' grocery bill. I never gave it a second thought until today. It dawned on me to compare each of the handwritten notes left on our storefront with the cash donations. You know, to see if they were written by the same person," Nellie explained.

"So, what were you able to determine?"

Nellie pointed at the writing. "Take a look for yourself. You can see all the handwriting looks the same."

"Yes, it appears that's the case." Cody rubbed his brow. "But I still don't know how this solves the mystery of who is actually our Secret Santa."

Nellie fished into her purse for the second time, pulling out another piece of paper. "Look at this." She handed it to Cody.

He examined the page. "What is this?"

"The other day while Hannah was in the store. I asked her

to make a list of some things she might need for her class-room. I thought it could be my gift for Christmas. You know the teachers purchase all of their supplies on their own, so I thought I could help out. This is a copy of the list she made for me."

Cody read through the list of supplies. The typical requests of pencils, art supplies, sticky notes and other miscellaneous items. "I'm still not following you. Why would this make you believe Hannah is the one behind all of the mysterious donations?"

Nellie grinned. "I don't think… I know for a fact. Just look at this." Nellie pointed to words written on the paper.

"What's that supposed to mean?"

"Look how some of the words have that extra curl in it." Nellie then pointed to the notes that had been left with the monetary donations. "See that. The same curliness is in these notes, particularly in the letter *s*. I'm telling you, Hannah is the town's Secret Santa."

Cody considered the results of Nellie's investigation. Could it be true? Was Hannah really behind all of the donations? Was that why she was acting peculiar today? It didn't make sense, though. Giving made people feel good. Today, she seemed sad about something. Besides, how could she afford so much? "Let's say you're right. How in the world would Hannah be in a position to make such generous contributions on a teacher's salary?"

"How much do you really know about Hannah? Has she been open with you about her past?" Nellie asked.

Since Cody first met Hannah, he wanted to know every-thing about her, but she wasn't open to sharing. Even when they were together at her house decorating the tree he had de-livered. Cody thought for sure it was the perfect opportunity for her to open up to him, but she hadn't. In the end, he was the only one who talked about his past that night.

"No, I don't know much about her. Any time I've tried to ask questions, she clams up."

Nellie nodded. "There's something she must be hiding. And my guess would be she is rich. How else could she afford to make the donations to the town and the Matthews family if she wasn't? Maybe she won the lottery?"

"I doubt that. Hannah doesn't strike me as the type who would play the lottery. Before you start to dream up all of these possibilities, keep in mind that we still don't know for sure that it's her." The last thing Cody wanted was for Nellie to start asking Hannah a bunch of questions. "Promise me you won't interrogate Hannah about her past. She might open up to me if I approach the subject carefully. We've been spending a lot of time together."

"I've noticed that. That's what's so surprising to me. You're so easy to talk to. You would be the first person I'd feel comfortable talking to about my past."

Cody smiled. "Thanks. I hadn't planned on telling you, but Hannah agreed to go with me as my date to the Christmas dance."

Nellie clapped her hands together. "Oh, that's wonderful news. Like I've said before, the two of you are meant for one another. Trust me. I know these things. I've predicted several weddings in this town and I have a feeling your and Hannah's marriage could be next."

"Whoa—hold on." Cody held up his hands. "I never said anything about proposing marriage. I simply invited her to the dance. And by the way, I haven't said anything to McKenzie and Madison about it yet, so I'd appreciate it if you could keep that between you and me."

"Of course. Mum's the word. This is so exciting! But I promise, I'll keep it to myself. Well, I'll tell Hank. I've never kept a secret from him in our sixty-five years of marriage."

"Hank is okay, but no one else." Cody looked across the

town square and spotted Hannah moving toward them, ferrying the tray of hot chocolates. "Shh…enough about the dance and your investigation. Here comes Hannah." He scooped up the pieces of paper strewn across the table. "Here, put these back inside of your purse."

Nellie followed Cody's instructions. "I'm going to leave the two of you alone. Let me know if you find out anything." She scurried off before Hannah made it to the table.

Cody's mind was swirling with possibilities. Was Nellie correct in believing Hannah is the Secret Santa? If so, where did she get the money? He'd have to be cautious with his approach, but he planned to get some answers after the snowman-making contest. If Hannah was keeping secrets about her past, they'd never have a chance at a possible future together.

Hannah's pace slowed when she observed Nellie and Cody huddled together, deep in conversation. Immediately after Cody looked in Hannah's direction, Nellie had hurriedly scooped up pieces of paper from the table and shoved them into her purse.

Hannah's stomach twisted. Had Nellie pieced together the puzzle and realized she was the one behind the donations? Were the scraps of paper scattered across the table the notes she'd left at the store? Was that what she was showing to Cody? She should have typed the notes, not written them by hand. Her heart slowed and her breathing became steady. Nellie didn't know what Hannah's handwriting looked like, right?

She continued to walk in Cody's direction and then she remembered. The gift Nellie planned to give Hannah's classroom for Christmas. Hannah had written, not typed, the list of school supplies.

Her chest tightened, causing her breaths to shorten. The panic attacks always started this way.

Breathe and calm down.

She continued to whisper to herself.

Don't let your imagination get the best of you.

Relax.

They would never guess.

On a teacher's salary...no way was that possible.

By the time Hannah reached the table, she'd successfully talked herself off the ledge and was breathing normally. "Four hot chocolates." She forced a smile.

Cody removed the tray from Hannah's grasp and placed it on the table. "Thank you."

"I got some for the twins, too."

"That was thoughtful of you." Cody glanced at his watch. "They should be heading this way any minute if Jake can peel them off the ice rink."

Hannah shifted her weight. Cody was looking at her funny. Or was it her imagination? Nope. He was. There was something about the way he said *ice rink*. Was he trying to see if she reacted to the mention of one of her donations? Or was she being paranoid?

"Are you okay?" Cody stepped closer and put his hand on her arm. "You look a little pale."

Hannah was far from okay—especially today. She'd made a big mistake by accepting his offer to drive her to the festival. Today of all days she needed to close the blinds in her house and stay underneath the covers until it was over. Instead, she'd put herself in a position where a panic attack in public almost felt inevitable, given the fact that it was the one-year anniversary of the tragedy that stole her family.

Hannah inhaled a deep breath. "I'm fine. I think it's probably my blood sugar. I was rushing around this morning and didn't eat breakfast." She tried to eat some toast, but even that had turned her stomach.

"Well, this sweet treat should do the trick for that."

Cody removed the lid from one of the cups and passed it to her. "Have a sip."

Hannah hoped Cody didn't notice how her hand shook when she accepted the beverage.

"Are you sure you're okay?"

Too late. She couldn't hide it. "Yes, I'm fine." Hannah moved the cup to her lips, willing her hand to stop shaking.

Cody kept a close eye on her.

"This is good." The creamy confection pumped through her bloodstream, but did little to settle her nerves. "I feel better already," she said, trying to convince him…and herself.

"Good." Cody looked around at the crowd of people lining up at the table. "We better get started. Most everyone has already signed up to participate. I think there's only a few stragglers."

"I can take care of them," Hannah offered, feeling more at ease.

Hannah placed her cup down and called out to the crowd. "Okay, those of you who have already registered can step over to the roped off area. The rest of you who need to sign up, please approach the table," she said, motioning to the sign-up sheet.

Everyone moved as instructed to the appropriate spot. She could do this. If she stayed busy, maybe she could make it through the day without drawing attention to herself by having a panic attack in the middle of the town square.

Just remember to breathe.

Later, the snowfall had increased in intensity, adding to the festive mood of the crowd. Snowmen of all shapes and sizes decorated the ground. The participants chattered among themselves as they waited for the judging to begin.

Hannah and Cody strolled from one snowman to the next. With their tablets in hand, they whispered to one another and made notes.

Hannah's heart rate had slowed while watching the construction take place. A few of the children started a snowball fight and the adults joined in, creating a fun and noncompetitive event. The creativity of the participants impressed both Hannah and Cody. Overall, the contest was a big success.

"That was so much fun!" McKenzie exclaimed.

"Yeah, even though we didn't win a prize it was so cool building our snowman while it was snowing." Madison skipped alongside Hannah and then reached for her hand. "Did you have fun, Miss Simpson?"

Hannah's heart squeezed at the feel of Madison's hand inside her own. "Yes, it was more fun than I've had in a long time."

"I'm glad. At first you didn't look like it." Madison looked up at Hannah.

"Yeah, I looked at you a couple of times and I thought you were crying," McKenzie added.

Hannah had done her best to try and conceal the pain she was experiencing, but apparently the twins were more observant than she'd realized.

"It was probably just the cold wind, right?" Cody looked at Hannah and winked.

She appreciated Cody's attempt to cover for her. It was apparent from the start of the contest that he sensed something was wrong. But being the gentleman that he was, Cody never questioned her or pushed for an answer. "Your uncle is right. I've always had problems with my eyes watering when I'm out in the cold for too long."

"Your eyes look a lot better now. Does that mean we can all go ice-skating together?" Madison asked.

Cody glanced at Hannah. Her skin tingled underneath her heavy coat.

"Yeah, can we, Uncle Cody? Can we all skate together like a real family?" McKenzie pleaded.

Family.

Hannah stopped in her tracks.

Thump, thump, thump.

Her heartbeat pounded against her eardrums.

No. Not here.

Not in front of the girls. She would scare them.

"Uncle Cody, what's wrong with her?" McKenzie looked up with her eyes filled with fear.

Cody approached Hannah.

Underneath her coat, her skin felt like it was on fire. She could feel the beads of sweat running down her back.

"Hannah?" Cody took her hand. "Are you all right?"

When she opened her mouth to speak, no words came.

"Is it your blood sugar again?" He guided her to a nearby bench. "Have a seat. I can go get Olivia, my sister-in-law."

"Yeah, she's the town doctor," Madison shared.

No.

The last thing Hannah wanted was a doctor. That could ruin her plan to start a new life where no one knew anything about her past.

"Hannah, can you hear me?" Cody got up in her face. She felt his breath. "Don't you want to sit?"

As much as she tried, Hannah couldn't get her legs to co-operate. Her field of vision narrowed while a trembling sensation moved from her hands up into her arms. Her breathing grew shallow.

"McKenzie, run and find Aunt Olivia for me!" Cody shouted.

"I'll get her fast." McKenzie took off running across the town square.

Hannah needed to leave before McKenzie returned with the doctor. But how? She was paralyzed. She couldn't walk. Even if she could, she didn't have a car. There was no way for her to escape.

"Try and breathe, Hannah. Olivia is a great doctor. She'll

be able to help you. If you can't sit down, just hold on to my arm. I won't let you fall."

The sound of Cody's voice soothed her enough to slow the trembling that radiated down into her legs. The strength was there to at least run away. She had no other choice. Otherwise, she'd be forced to share her past with everyone listening.

A second later, Hannah pulled her hand away from Cody's grip and ran.

"Hannah, wait!" Cody yelled, but didn't attempt to follow her.

With no particular direction in mind at first, just a primal need to escape—Hannah bolted. Her boots provided enough traction to run across the snow-covered ground. Then she remembered the hot chocolate. If she could make it to Garrison's Mercantile, Hank was manning the kiosk. She could tell him she wasn't feeling well and ask him to drive her home. He wouldn't ask a lot of questions. Hank wasn't like Nellie. He was a quiet man. Hank would keep her secret.

Chapter Thirteen

Cody questioned each step as he crept up the front stairs of Hannah's house. He didn't know for sure that she'd even returned home following her abrupt departure after the snowman-making contest. If she had, would she even open the door and talk to him? He couldn't help but be reminded of the day she'd run away once before, leaving him with questions.

Earlier at the festival, after Olivia showed up, Cody had explained Hannah's behavior. Olivia's first thought was that it sounded like a panic attack.

Upon reaching the door, he gently knocked. When there was no answer, he knocked a second time. She had to be inside. Where else could she have gone?

Inside, the sound of footsteps reached the foyer. Then Hannah peered out the window before opening the door. "Cody, what are you doing here?"

Cody was taken back by Hannah's bedraggled look. Hannah was much like Olivia when it came to her outer appearance. "I wanted to make sure you made it home okay. You left so suddenly. I was worried about you."

Hannah pulled the door open wider and stepped aside. "Come inside. It's too cold for you to stand there. Excuse my appearance. I've been doing some housework." She motioned him into the foyer.

This was progress. After the way Hannah took off, he wasn't

sure if she would let him come into the house. He'd decided on his drive over that he wasn't going to leave until he learned what was going on with her. If she was experiencing panic attacks like Olivia thought, what was triggering them?

"Thank you." Cody came in the door and heard Christmas carols streaming through the speakers in the family room. The lights were turned off, but the Christmas tree lights illuminated the space.

"Can I get you something hot to drink?" Hannah pushed her tangled mass of hair away from her face.

"A cup of coffee sounds great. The snow is still coming down." He stomped his feet on the front mat to knock away the snow.

"Let me take your coat and I'll get us a cup." She reached for his outerwear and hung it on the coatrack in the corner of the foyer. "You can go ahead into the family room and turn on the lights, if you'd like."

Despite her appearance, Hannah sounded different than she had a couple of hours ago. Now she was calm and her hands appeared steady. Cody hoped it was a good sign. Perhaps she would finally be ready to talk to him. Though they'd been spending a lot of time together, she felt like a stranger to him. He knew nothing about her life before moving to Bluebell Canyon.

Cody stepped into the family room and stopped to notice the tree. The evening he'd brought it over and told Hannah about his past relationship, he'd felt something shift between them. Had it only been his imagination or did she feel for him the way he felt for her?

Sounds of dishes clanking came from the kitchen. Cody was walking closer to the tree when he kicked something on the floor. He bent over and picked up a framed photograph. In the picture, Hannah stood arm in arm with a handsome man. Standing in front of them was a little girl with a bright smile.

She looked exactly like Hannah. Was this part of Hannah's past? A piece she didn't want to share with him?

"Here we go. I hope the coffee isn't too strong for you for this hour of the day." Hannah carried the two cups into the room.

Cody flinched.

Hannah's eyes traveled to his hands. "What are you doing with that?" Her tone was much different than earlier.

"It was on the floor. I almost stepped on it." He gently placed it on the mantel next to another photo of what looked like could be Hannah's parents. "I only picked it up to move it out of the way."

Hannah's face was void of expression.

"I don't want to pry into your life or make you upset, but I hope you'll share with me who these people are." Cody stepped closer, but Hannah moved away and snatched the frame from where Cody had placed it.

"You can't upset me more than I already am." She brushed away a tear. "This is my family."

Hannah had a family? Why hadn't she ever mentioned this to him? "Wow. I guess I'd been wrong to assume there was something developing between us. I suppose your accepting my invitation to the dance was just a friendly gesture on your part."

Hannah slowly shook her head. "Maybe I need to clarify something." Hannah inhaled a deep breath and expelled it. "This is difficult for me to talk about."

Cody noticed her hands began to tremble again, like they had earlier after the snowman-making contest. He fixed his gaze on her. "Like I said before, the last thing I want to do is upset you, but I would really like to know what's going on here." He raked his hand through his hair, shaking his head.

"I should have told you before now. I wanted to—honestly, I really did, but it's so difficult to talk about." Hannah dragged her feet to the sofa, still holding the picture. She took a seat. "Will you sit with me?" She patted her hand on the cushion.

Cody moved toward her and sat down. His stomach twisted, not sure what he was about to hear, but he wanted to make it as easy as possible for Hannah. It was obvious she was suffering from a great deal of emotional turmoil. He took her hand. "Take as long as you need. I'm not going anywhere."

Hannah nodded slowly and traced her finger across the glass of the picture frame. "This *was* my family. That's Rick. He was my husband." She paused and swallowed. "And this is Jenna, my daughter."

Cody wasn't prepared for this. He remained silent.

"It was a year ago today that they both died." Hannah's voice remained surprisingly calm and direct.

Cody's chest tightened. "I'm so sorry." His voice crackled. He couldn't put Hannah through the pain of reliving the horrible tragedy…especially not on the anniversary of the event. "You don't have to say any more."

"No, believe it or not, just admitting that to you feels like a tremendous weight has been lifted off of my shoulders. I've really wanted to talk to someone, particularly today, but my best friend and old coworker who lives in Phoenix is out of the country."

"Okay then. Just pretend I'm your friend." Cody smiled to lighten the mood. "I'm going to keep quiet. You tell me as much or as little as you like." He gave her hand a squeeze. "Anytime you want to stop or you'd like for me to leave, just let me know."

Hannah placed the photograph on the coffee table and picked up her cup of coffee. She wrapped her fingers around the cup and stared at the Christmas tree before taking a sip of the beverage. "I was away on a retreat with some of my colleagues from school. I was due to come home the next day when I got a call from our neighbor."

Hannah hesitated for several seconds. She glanced at the

photo. "There was a carbon monoxide leak in the heating system overnight. Our annual maintenance appointment for the furnace had been scheduled in early November, but we had to cancel it to leave town for a funeral. Neither Rick nor I remembered to reschedule. The night of the accident, the temperature was predicted to drop to an unseasonable low. Rick must have decided to turn on the heat so Jenna wouldn't get too cold while she slept. Neither of them woke up the next morning."

Cody was speechless. What could he say to help ease the pain? He took both of her hands and held them. "I'm so sorry, Hannah. I wish I'd known this sooner."

"When I moved to Bluebell Canyon, I didn't want anyone to know about my past. Moving here was a way for me to have a fresh start. Where people wouldn't look at me with pity or feel uncomfortable around me. But keeping it bottled up hasn't been good for me."

"I'm guessing that's why you're experiencing panic attacks?" Cody asked.

Hannah pulled her hands away. "How did you know?"

"I had an idea that's what was going on after you took off from the festival. I spoke with Olivia. She confirmed based on what I described to her."

Hannah hung her head. "I'm so embarrassed."

"No, don't be. I didn't bring this up to cause you embarrassment. I know how debilitating panic attacks can be."

"For a while they weren't happening as frequently. The closer it got to the anniversary, I started to have them more often. I don't want to jeopardize my job by having one in the classroom and frightening the children."

"I don't think you have to worry about your job security. From what I hear around town, everyone loves you," Cody said, smiling.

"Thank you for listening to me. I'll admit, it feels better not keeping it a secret any longer."

Cody nodded and placed his arm around her, wishing he could help to ease her pain.

Hannah was visibly exhausted from sharing her past. For the next half hour, Cody held her while they listened to soft Christmas music while the Christmas tree lights twinkled. Maybe there was a way he could help Hannah. But would she be receptive to his suggestion? Probably not. With Christmas right around the corner, perhaps there was an even better way.

Late the following Saturday afternoon, Hannah cranked up the volume on her tablet and danced around the kitchen to "Jingle Bell Rock." Her heart buzzed with excitement. Tonight was the big finale of the festival. And best of all, Cody was her date to the Christmas dance.

The culmination of activities held last weekend, along with last night's festivities, prompted the mayor to send an early morning email to both her and Cody. In the message, he commended both for stepping up to the plate at the last minute and putting together an event that the town wouldn't forget. He thanked them for their hard work and asked if she and Cody would be willing to volunteer again next year.

Neither she nor Cody responded to the email. At least, she hadn't. If Cody responded, he didn't copy her on his reply. Reading the message in the early morning hours while enjoying her morning coffee sent Hannah's mind into a daydreaming state filled with a lot of questions. What would her life be like a year from now? Would her panic attacks become less frequent? Would Cody be a part of her future? During her recent prayer time, a still, small voice told her it was time to open her heart to the possibility of a future that maybe included Cody.

After opening up to him last weekend, Hannah felt a tremendous weight lift from her shoulders. During the past week, Hannah spent time with Cody helping to train Ellie. The dog had come a long way since Hannah first met her. Cody expressed it was only a matter of time before she would be ready to begin her life as a service animal. Hannah didn't want to think about the day she'd have to say goodbye to Ellie.

The tea kettle heating on the stove whistled at the same time her cell phone alerted her to a new text message. Hannah removed the kettle and poured the boiling water into the candy cane mug containing a peppermint tea bag. As the tea steeped, she picked up her cell phone to check the text message. A part of her hoped it was from Cody.

With two taps, the message opened. Her heart slowed when she realized it wasn't from Cody as she'd hoped, but a delivery confirmation. The computer she'd ordered for the Matthews family had been delivered. Hannah smiled. Now Mary's mother, Joyce, could once again resume working from home to help the family with their monthly expenses.

Hannah no sooner deleted the confirmation before another text came through. This one prompted an even bigger smile.

Looking forward to tonight. C xo

Hannah's insides tingled at the thought of spending the evening dancing in Cody's arms.

Before she had an opportunity to reply to the first message, a second one came through.

I have no idea what to wear. C xo

Cody's words sparked a laugh. She was relieved she wasn't the only one with wardrobe worries. That morning, Hannah had stood in front of her closet waiting for the perfect outfit to jump out at her. After spending two hours trying on multiple pairs of pants with matching sweater possibilities, a dozen different skirts and dresses, Hannah remembered Nellie mentioning that in years past the attire was typically casual. She said there wasn't a woman in Bluebell Canyon who would expose their bare legs to the harsh winter elements at an outdoor event. With additional snow in the forecast for tonight, along with gusty winds, Hannah followed Nellie's suggestion. She decided to wear winter-white corduroy pants paired with a cable-knit sweater of the same color.

You'll look good in anything. H

Hannah's message lingered on the screen, her finger hovering over the send button. Was this response a little too forward? Following a moment of contemplation, she added *xo* and hit Send.

Cody's response came immediately, giving her little time for regret.

With you by my side, no one will notice me. C xo

Hannah responded with a smiley face. Then the little dots moved, indicating Cody was typing another message. Her pulse raced in anticipation of what he might say next.

Since the forecast is calling for more snow, we'll pick you up. Can you be ready by six thirty? C xo

Hannah rolled her neck back and forth, relaxing in the knowledge that someone cared about her safety. Since losing her husband, she'd missed that feeling. She quickly typed a response.

I'll be ready. Thank you for being so considerate.

Cody's response was immediate.

Only for you. C xo

* * *

Three hours later, the cold nipped at Hannah's cheeks as she and Cody walked hand in hand along the Walk of Lights. "Silent Night" spread melodic holiday cheer, thanks to Cody's idea of an outdoor sound system.

"Your idea to have music was brilliant."

"But the walk of lights was your idea. We make a good team." Cody smiled and looked around. "It does sound nice, doesn't it. At least we didn't waste money on a snowmaking machine."

"Yes, Mother Nature's timing has been next to perfect these past two weekends." Hannah bent down with her gloved hand and scooped up some snow before playfully tossing it at Cody's chest.

"You don't know who you're messing with, do you?" Cody repeated Hannah's earlier action and scooped some snow off the ground, but instead of throwing it, he packed it into a perfectly shaped ball. "I hold the long-standing record for winning the most snowball fights back in my hometown of Whispering Slopes."

"Oh, do you now?" She glanced at the hot chocolate kiosk outside of Garrison's Mercantile. "Well then, why don't we forego the fight and grab a cup of hot chocolate instead?" Hannah suggested.

"Chicken." Cody playfully nudged Hannah before taking her hand again and leading her across the street.

As they approached Garrison's Mercantile, Hannah watched Nellie flash a bright smile and tug on her husband's arm. She pointed to Hannah and Cody. Nellie's eyes never pulled away from the couple's interlocked hands.

"Hey you two." Hank spoke first.

"Can we get two large cups—" Cody glanced at Hannah "—with extra marshmallows?"

Hannah quickly shook her head in agreement. "Yes, definitely."

Hank went to work on the order while Nellie moved closer to Hannah.

"Seeing the two of you together is the best Christmas present I could hope for." Nellie placed her hand to her heart. "I've prayed for this."

Cody grinned and wrapped his arm around Hannah's shoulders. "It looks like both of our prayers have been answered."

Hannah's heart melted knowing Cody had prayed for the same. After opening up to Cody and revealing her past, the fear eased. Keeping a secret could be noble in some situations, but when it came to her personal life, Hannah had learned full disclosure was what God wanted from her. "Mine too," she added as she accepted the cup from Hank.

"Are you guys going to shut down the kiosk and join everyone at the dance?" Cody asked.

"With this weather, we've had a steady stream of customers. We thought we could leave it open and allow everyone to help themselves." Hank wrapped his arm around Nellie's waist. "I don't want to deprive anyone of their hot chocolate fix, but there's no way I'm going to miss out on dancing with my bride tonight."

Nellie blushed and nuzzled against her husband. "After all of these years, he's still the most romantic man I've ever known."

That's what Hannah wanted again. A second chance at the kind of love Hank and Nellie had. A love that she once had with Rick, but lost way too soon. God had brought Cody into her life in His own perfect timing. Was she ready to take the risk?

"Miss Simpson!"

Hannah turned at the sound of a child's voice and spotted Mary Matthews walking down the sidewalk holding hands with her parents, Joe and Joyce.

The family stepped up to the kiosk, all smiles.

"We'll take three hot chocolates, Nellie." Joe put in his order as he reached for his wallet.

Hank held up his hand. "Put your money away. Tonight the hot chocolate is free. Nellie and I were just getting ready to head over to the pavilion."

Hannah looked down at Mary. "Are you enjoying your Christmas vacation so far?"

"Yeah, but I've missed you and my friends. I'm glad everyone will be here tonight." Mary smiled up at her mother. "Especially you, Mommy."

Joyce bent down and hugged her daughter. "I'm happy too, honey."

"We're celebrating tonight and rejoicing in a double blessing from God. Joyce had her last treatment yesterday, and my doctor cleared me to go back to work in the middle of January," Joe said, smiling.

Hannah's heart was full as everyone cheered and congratulated the family.

"I see McKenzie, Madison and some other kids over there," Mary said, pointing. "Can I go say hi, Daddy?"

"Your mother and I wanted to speak with Miss Simpson for a second."

Nellie stepped forward and took Mary's hand. "Hank and I will take her, if that's okay. You two stay and talk with Hannah."

"Thank you, Nellie." Joyce leaned down and kissed her daughter.

Hank and Nellie accompanied Mary toward the twins, who were busy building a snowman with a group of their classmates.

Joe stepped closer to Hannah. "My wife and I wanted to say thank you for all that you've done to help our family."

Hannah bit her lip. "I'm not sure what you're referring to."

"Would you like for me to leave you all alone?" Cody slipped his hands into the pockets of his coat.

Without hesitation, Joe rested his hand on Cody's shoulder. "We'd rather you stay. There's something you should know about this lady you've been keeping company with lately." Joe grinned.

Hannah prepared herself for what Joe was going to say.

"It took a while to figure out who was blessing us each week with groceries. We grilled Nellie, but she swore she had no idea. And then we were blessed with money to help with our medical bills." Joe placed his hand on Hannah's arm. "We know that you've been our Secret Santa this year. We understand you wanted to keep your identity a secret, but we couldn't not acknowledge your generosity."

Despite the cold temperature, Hannah's face grew warm.

Joyce moved closer and wrapped her arms tight around Hannah. "We trusted God to take care of us during this challenging time and in His always perfect timing, He brought you into our lives. We can never thank you enough, Hannah." Joyce stepped away and wiped the tears flowing down her cheeks.

Hannah's eyes moistened. "You're welcome. But may I ask how you knew it was me?"

Cody spoke first. "I'm curious, too. Even Nellie didn't have a clue and we all know nothing gets past her."

The group laughed.

Joyce turned to her husband. "Maybe you should explain."

Hannah did everything she could to cover all of her tracks.

"The computer delivered today tipped us off. It was the connecting piece of the puzzle," Joe explained.

When she placed the order for the computer, Hannah hadn't included any message that would trace the gift back to her.

"I'm still confused." Cody scratched the bottom of his chin.

"When we first opened the box, we didn't know who it was from. Then Mary came home from the neighbor's house and saw the computer. She told us Miss Simpson sent it." Joe looked at Hannah. "You were the only one who knew our old computer had died, which meant Joyce could no longer work remotely."

Hannah nodded. The moment she'd heard the news, she realized what a devastating blow it was to the Matthews family. They relied on Joyce's income, especially since Joe wasn't able to work due to his knee injury. "Yes, on the last day of school before Christmas break, Mary seemed upset. I asked her to stay after class. She told me about the computer."

"You have no idea what a saving grace it was to us. Joyce was afraid she would lose her job. Instead, she received a gift from you that will enable her to keep her job, along with a Christmas bonus from her company. I don't know how we will ever repay you for your kindness." Now it was Joe's turn to wipe his tears.

Hannah shook her head. "You already have. I thought doing all of this in secret was the best way to help you. But seeing your appreciation firsthand has been a wonderful gift to me."

Cody glanced at his watch. "We better get over to the pavilion. The dance is scheduled to begin any minute and we're in charge of the music." He took Hannah's hand. "Shall we?"

As the couples strolled down the sidewalk lined with twinkling lights, a peaceful feeling came over Hannah. But as quick as it appeared, a sudden and overwhelming feeling of anxiousness squeezed her lungs. Why was this happening now? She no longer held any secrets. What was the trigger? Hannah did her best to steady her breathing while she questioned whether or not the panic attacks would ever cease and she could find peace once again.

Chapter Fourteen

❧

"You didn't know I'd be such a good dancer, did you?" Cody joked and passed Hannah a cup of punch. The disc jockey had taken his second and last break of the evening before the big fireworks display was scheduled to begin in under one hour.

It thrilled Cody to see Hannah enjoying herself again. After Joe and Joyce had revealed Hannah's identity as the town's Secret Santa, he'd noticed signs of an impending panic attack as they made their way to the pavilion holding hands. Much like the previous attack Cody had witnessed, Hannah's face flushed and her breathing appeared labored. This time, Cody kept quiet, allowing her to regain her normal breathing. Seeing this only reinforced the idea he had for Hannah's Christmas gift.

Hannah quickly glanced at her feet before tossing a wink at Cody. "It's a good thing I didn't wear open-toed shoes tonight."

"I never stepped on your toes." Cody smiled sheepishly. "Well, maybe once or twice. I probably shouldn't have worn these heavy cowboy boots."

"It's been a wonderful evening so far…definitely worth a couple of sore toes," Hannah giggled.

"I'll try to do better under two conditions."

Hannah's eyebrow arched. "Two? I'm anxious to hear."

"First, you have to promise the remaining dances of the night to me."

"So far, you're the only man I've danced with, so that shouldn't be too hard. What's the second condition?"

"A confession." Cody watched as Hannah's expression went blank. "Since you've been exposed as the town's Secret Santa, is it safe for me to assume you also made all of the generous donations for the festival?" Cody gazed into Hannah's eyes. "Am I right?"

Hannah gave a slight nod. "I planned to tell you. After you learned about my panic attacks, I made the decision that I didn't want any more secrets between us. I'm sorry I didn't tell you sooner."

Cody sensed Hannah's guilt. "Hey, wait." He took her hand. "There's no need to apologize. You've been so generous to our town. Not only with your money, but with your time and compassion for others. I wanted to say thank you for all you've done."

Tears streamed down Hannah's creamy complexion. "I'm thankful to God that I was able to turn a painful event in my life into something good."

Cody remained silent, unsure of what Hannah's words meant.

"Let me explain. My husband sold insurance for a living, so it goes without saying he was heavily insured, along with my daughter. When they both passed, the insurance claims paid out more money than I could ever spend in my lifetime."

Cody hadn't said anything to Nellie or anyone else in town, but he wondered how Hannah could afford everything she'd done for the Matthews family on a teacher's salary. This explained a lot.

"Until I moved to Bluebell Canyon, I hadn't touched any of the money. Besides being a constant reminder of what I'd lost, it just didn't feel right. The people in this town, yourself included, have taught me that life can indeed go on after loss. That God wants me to enjoy my life and the favor He provides me with each day. Giving back to this community has helped me to heal."

Hearing Hannah say this gave him hope that perhaps there was a chance for the two of them to pursue a relationship. Maybe he could let go of his own wrong mindset when it came to his insecurities, particularly when it came to dating. "Well, thank you for all that you've done to make this the most memorable festival for the town—and for me as well."

The joyous sounds of the townspeople celebrating the season filled the air.

"Try the punch. Let me know what you think," Cody suggested.

"Yum…this is delicious. What is this? It tastes like apple cider, but there's something different." She took another sip of the spicy beverage.

"I'm not sure. Nellie came up with the recipe a few years ago. It's been a big hit at the festival each year." Cody took a drink. "Speaking of Nellie. Did she invite you over for Christmas dinner?" He couldn't imagine Nellie not extending an invitation to Hannah. It appeared the two had become good friends.

While they'd worked with Ellie earlier in the week, Hannah hadn't mentioned any plans. Cody didn't want her to spend the day alone, but maybe she planned on flying to Phoenix to visit friends. Either way, Cody had to know so he could decide on the perfect time to gift her his Christmas surprise.

"Nellie did invite me, but I'm not sure if I'm going."

"Do you have a better offer?" For a second, Cody's mind reeled. Was Caleb still trying to date Hannah?

"No, I just thought the dinner would be more family oriented. I'm not sure I want to feel like the odd man out, being the only single woman attending."

"You don't have to worry about that. I'm going and I'm single."

"Yes, but you'll be with McKenzie and Madison." Hannah stubbed the toe of her boot into the snow.

"Are you kidding? With Jake's and Logan's kids there, I'll be left alone." Cody stepped closer to Hannah, causing his pulse to quicken. "Why don't you and I go together?"

Hannah's face appeared flushed. "Like a date?"

Cody took her hand in his own. "Not like—I'm talking about a real date," he whispered against her ear. "I'll pick you up and everything. Only this time, I won't be picking you up because the roads are too dangerous for you to drive."

"Imagine what Nellie will think."

"I am." Cody flashed a mischievous grin. "She'll be reserving the church for our wedding."

They both laughed.

"Seriously, will you be my date for Christmas?" Cody held his breath, not sure how Hannah would answer.

"There's nothing more I'd rather do." Hannah answered the exact moment the music resumed. She glanced toward the dance floor. "Except maybe dance with you to this song. It's one of my favorites."

"No way," Cody exclaimed.

Hannah's smile disappeared and her brow wrinkled.

"I mean…it's my favorite song, too." Cody removed the cup from her hands and placed it on a nearby table before discarding his own drink. "Let's dance, shall we?"

Forty-five minutes later, the last song of the night came way too soon for Cody. He didn't want the evening to come to an end, but he was thankful the final song choice gave him the opportunity to hold Hannah close. Earlier in the evening, following their first slow dance, Cody had sent up a silent prayer for more.

"This is nice," Cody whispered in Hannah's ear. Thanks to the overhead heaters inside the pavilion, they both had removed their coats during one of the faster dances. Cody felt Hannah's heartbeat against his chest.

Hannah nuzzled her face against Cody's cheek. "I agree. I'm not ready for it to end."

"Why does it have to?" This was his opportunity. If not now—when? "I don't only mean this dance or the night. I'm talking about our time together. These past several weeks have been some of the happiest times I can remember. I don't want it to end after the holidays." Cody released a long and noticeable breath. "Phew…that felt good to finally say."

The music stopped but Cody held on to Hannah while their bodies continued to sway. Without warning, the sky exploded in flashes of red, green, white and blue. The fireworks marking the end of the festival had begun.

Hannah gazed at the sky before turning her eyes back to Cody. "I don't want this to end either," she whispered.

Cody's pulse responded as he drew Hannah closer. The sweetness of her breath against his face and the softness of her feminine frame caused him to throw caution to the wind. He lightly brushed his lips across her mouth. When she didn't protest, he realized this was only the beginning.

Two days before Christmas, Hannah scurried down the sidewalk. Fat snowflakes splattered against her face. With a shopping list tucked inside of her purse, she headed toward Garrison's Mercantile to pick up a few items. The plan to stay home today to bake cookies along with wrapping a few gifts was squashed once she realized she was out of eggs.

As she neared the Hummingbird Café, the enticing aroma of freshly brewed coffee teased Hannah's senses. Caffeine. That would give her the boost she needed to work through the extensive to-do list waiting for her at home.

Hannah stepped inside the establishment. A comforting warmth settled her racing mind.

"Hi, Hannah." Sally poked her head up from behind the counter as she filled the pastry case with fresh doughnuts.

"I'm beginning to think you have a bedroom in your back room," Hannah joked. "I thought the upside of being a business owner is hiring other people to do all of the work." Hannah approached Sally and pulled the red scarf from around her neck.

Sally wiped her hands down her apron decorated with tiny hummingbirds. "Honestly, I wouldn't know what to do with myself if I wasn't here every day."

Hannah could relate. She felt the same way about her job as a teacher.

"What can I get you?"

"When you have a chance, I'll take a large espresso to go."

"You got it." Sally turned and headed to the kitchen.

Hannah took a seat and her eyes panned the crowded room. Several servers buzzed around the space refilling cups and taking orders.

Moments later, Hannah's breath hitched when she heard the familiar laugh. Cody. He was sitting at a corner table next to the fireplace…but he wasn't alone.

"Here you go, sweetie." Sally passed the foam cup over the counter.

Hannah's words seemed frozen somewhere between her brain and her mouth. She squeezed the cup in her hands. Only last night, she and Cody had shared their first kiss.

"Thank you." Her voice cracked. "Sally, who is that woman with Cody?"

Sally turned to the attractive brunette sitting with Cody at a table by the fireplace. She placed her hand to her face. "I'm not sure. They must have come in while I was busy with the delivery truck out back."

Underneath Hannah's feet, the floor seemed to sway. The scarf she removed earlier, still tossed aside on the stool next to her, felt like it was tightening around her throat. Her eyes locked with Cody's. Beads of sweat trickled down her back.

Hannah sprang from the stool, still clutching the cup. "I have to go." She spun on her heel to make her escape.

Air.

She couldn't breathe.

She had to make it outside before the entire café witnessed the panic attack.

"Hannah!" Cody's voice trailed behind her.

Finally at the front entrance, Hannah lunged against the door. The bell overhead sounded like massive wind chimes caught in a tornado.

Once outside, Hannah dropped her coffee cup and clutched the wrought iron railing that surrounded the porch. She shivered as the cold air mingled with the sweat underneath her coat.

"Hannah, are you okay?" Cody's voice calmed her racing pulse only moments after she'd stepped outside. He moved toward her with fear in his eyes.

Cody reached inside of his pocket. He removed a piece of peppermint gum. "I thought it was a good idea to start carrying this with me...just in case."

Their fingers brushed when Hannah accepted the gum. Her labored breathing eased. "Thank you." She unwrapped the stick and placed it on her tongue. The cooling sensation relaxed her mind. "I chewed my last piece yesterday. It's on my list to buy today."

With a gentle touch, Cody took Hannah's hand, picked up her spilled coffee cup and tossed it into the trash can. He guided Hannah to the cedar bench on the far side of the wrap-around porch. "Let's sit here for a minute."

Hannah followed his lead and took a seat. The threat of a full-blown panic attack had passed. "The gum helped," she said, smiling.

Cody leaned forward, placing his elbows on his thighs. He turned to face her. "Why did you run away when I called your name? I wanted you to join us."

"I didn't want to interrupt your date." Hannah tucked a strand of hair behind her ear, avoiding eye contact.

Cody laughed out loud. "Is that why you took off? You thought I was on a date?" He slid closer and placed his hand under her chin, gently tilting her head in his direction. "After last night? You thought I'd go out on a date with another woman?"

Hannah shook her head. "I didn't know what else to think."

"The woman at the table is Londyn Wentworth. She's an old high school classmate of my brother. She flew from Virginia to Denver this morning. Londyn and her two younger sisters also train service animals. They have plans to expand their business. Londyn came to take a look at our operation. Since everyone in Jake's house has a stomach bug, I told him I'd meet with her."

Hannah slouched forward and wrapped her arms around her waist. Why did she suspect the worst and run out like a jealous teenager? "I can't imagine what you must think of me…"

Cody placed his arm around Hannah and pulled her close.

Hannah settled into the nook beneath his arm and looked up.

Cody's hazel eyes gleamed as he moved in closer. He brushed his lips against hers, leaving her breathless. "You want to know what I think?"

Hannah's eyes closed and she shook her head.

"Look at me."

Hannah complied.

"I think you're pretty cute when you're jealous."

They both laughed and held one another for several minutes before Cody stood. He extended a hand to Hannah. "Come inside. I'd like for you to meet Londyn."

Hannah maintained her composure after the kiss left her

longing for more. "I'd like that, too." She rose from the bench. Her cell phone chimed a new text message and her watch vibrated. She glanced at the screen on her wrist. It was her best friend and fellow teacher, Lisa. The subject line read Urgent... call me!

"If you need to get that, you can meet us inside," Cody said.

"I don't want to be rude, but it's my friend and old coworker from Phoenix. We taught at the same school. She's back in the country. Her text said it's urgent." Hannah rubbed her lips with her index finger.

"Take your time. I'll order you a new coffee." Cody lightly touched her arm before heading inside.

Following a brief conversation with Lisa, Hannah ended the call. The reason her friend reached out left Hannah's mind reeling. The principal at the school where Hannah had taught planned to take an early retirement due to an illness. But that hadn't been the only reason for Lisa's urgent text. During an emergency meeting, the school board unanimously voted to offer the vacant principal position to Hannah.

Her heart raced as she slowly moved across the porch. Since entering the education field, Hannah believed the end goal was to one day become a principal. She opened the door of the café and spotted Cody. The man who was helping her to put the pieces of her broken life back together. Meeting someone like him following the tragedy that changed her life forever was something she never dreamed could happen. Could she walk away from a possible future with Cody?

Chapter Fifteen

Cody was up early on Christmas Eve morning only to discover Mother Nature had gifted the town of Bluebell Canyon an early present. With a couple of inches of snow on the ground and the intensity lessening, traveling to church this evening shouldn't be a problem.

Relaxing by the fireplace with a cup of coffee and Hershey napping on her bed next to the hearth, Cody's first thought was to call Hannah and offer to pick her up tonight. He didn't want her driving on icy roads. It was only five in the morning, so he'd have to wait. But that didn't stop Cody's thoughts from remaining on Hannah. What if she declined his offer to join him and the girls at Christmas Eve service?

Yesterday, following the incident at the café, Cody believed all was well after the misunderstanding concerning Londyn. Yet, once Hannah had come inside after speaking with her friend Lisa, she appeared distant. Of course, she'd been cordial when he'd introduced the two women, but even after Londyn left to head back to Denver to catch her flight, something was different about Hannah. He didn't even have the opportunity to mention the church service tonight.

Cody's cell phone sounded an alert, pulling him from his thoughts. Hershey's head popped up from the pillow. "It's okay, girl. Go back to sleep." The dog obeyed the command.

Cody rose from his chair and proceeded to the kitchen. Fortunately, he had the volume turned on low, so it didn't wake up the girls. With gifts still left to wrap, he didn't want them to wake up too early this morning.

Mindlessly, he refilled his coffee before picking up the cell phone. As expected, it was a weather update. The snow was moving out and temperatures were predicted to rise.

This was good news. A little snow on Christmas was always nice, especially for the kids, but this storm wasn't enough to force a change of plans. That would mean he'd hopefully see Hannah.

Hannah's behavior yesterday had Cody rethinking his original plan for her gift. Perhaps she could use a little early Christmas cheer. He had planned to present the gift when he picked her up to take her to the Garrisons for Christmas dinner. With excitement building when he thought about how she would respond, Cody wasn't sure he could wait.

After pacing the kitchen with his cup of coffee, he came up with a revised plan. Since he hadn't told the girls about his special gift for Hannah, out of fear they might spill the beans, he'd give Logan a call. If it was okay with him and Caitlyn, he'd drop the girls off and head over to Hannah's house, if he got the green light from her.

With a quick check of the radar on his phone, Cody noticed the precipitation would be long gone by noon. Perfect. That would give him plenty of time to wrap the Christmas gifts, get the girls their breakfast and hopefully drop them off at Logan's house. He'd wait until after nine o'clock to text Hannah.

Several hours later, McKenzie and Madison were up and pacing the kitchen floor like caged animals.

"When can we go out and play in the snow?" McKenzie pressed her nose against the glass on the French door. "The sun is already out. It's going to melt."

Cody put the last of the breakfast dishes into the dishwasher and pressed the start button. "You both need to brush your teeth and get your snowsuits on first." Before he turned from the counter the girls zipped out of the kitchen like two hummingbirds. Hershey raced to catch up, nipping at their heels.

No time like the present. Cody slipped his cell phone from his pocket. He'd been dying to text Hannah since his feet first hit the floor this morning.

Good morning! Happy Christmas Eve day! C xo

Cody stood frozen, waiting for a response from Hannah.

A minute passed, feeling like an eternity. Maybe she'd slept in this morning.

Cody busied himself cleaning up the kitchen, but he couldn't get his mind off Hannah.

When his phone beeped, announcing a text, he held his breath as he tapped the screen.

Same to you.

Unable to read anything into her response, Cody quickly typed another message.

I thought I would stop by for a quick visit today...if that's okay.

With her brief reply earlier, Cody decided to forego the *xo*. He waited in anticipation as the tiny dots moved, telling him she was typing.

Sorry, but I have a lot to do before church tonight.

Okay. Maybe she hadn't finished her baking or wrapping gifts. That was understandable, although disappointing.

I understand. Can the girls and I swing by and give you a ride to the church? I know you don't like driving when the roads are bad.

The sun is out over here. I'm sure the roads will be fine. Maybe I'll see you there.

A shiver rattled his core. Cody read the response a second time. No, he hadn't misunderstood. Hannah was blowing him off…but why?

The girls thundered down the steps, full of energy and girlish giggles. Cody's shoulders slumped as he slid his cell phone back into his pocket. Something was definitely up with Hannah. But he couldn't push her. No doubt the first holiday without her family was difficult. As much as he wanted to be there and help her to get through the holiday season, it might be best to give her the space she needs.

"We're ready to go outside, Uncle Cody!" the twins announced in unison as they skipped into the kitchen dressed in their neon pink snowsuits.

Cody's heart melted. What a gift these girls were to him.

"Can we go sledding on the big hill at Uncle Logan's house?" McKenzie asked.

Cody couldn't allow the situation with Hannah to put a damper on the twins' Christmas, especially after such a successful festival. He and the girls had a great time together and he'd realized something. Being a father was what he truly wanted. It wasn't only a matter of fulfilling his best friend's last wish. Cody loved McKenzie and Madison as though they were his own. He wanted to spend every Christmas with them…as their father. He hadn't shared his decision with his brothers. The truth was, Cody wanted to share it with Hannah first. But given her chilly response to his text message, had he been foolish to think they could have a chance at a future together?

* * *

Hannah purposely arrived at church two minutes before the service was scheduled to start. She'd grown up in the church, so she was aware of the crowds on Christmas Eve. It was when all of the people who never attended services during the year made their appearance.

As Hannah expected and hoped, the church was full. Her goal was to slip in unnoticed.

She settled into the back pew next to an elderly couple she didn't recognize. They both smiled before turning their attention to the altar lined with candles.

A quick scan of the sanctuary showed no sign of Cody and the girls. She spotted Nellie and Hank toward the front of the church. Strange. Cody and the twins typically sat up front with the Garrisons.

The organist began to play "Away in a Manger," causing an ache to consume her heart. She'd handled everything wrong earlier today. Why did she reject Cody's offer to pay her a visit? Maybe allowing him to come to her house would have been better. They could have talked about her behavior following her conversation with Lisa. Then Hannah could have explained about the job offer. Was it really better to run into him here or at the Garrisons' house for the first time and be forced to explain her behavior in front of others? That wasn't fair to Cody…but it was too late now.

"Miss Simpson!" McKenzie whispered, but loud enough for most of the congregation to turn and look.

"Shh…sit down," Cody instructed the girls as the two scooched in beside Hannah. Cody took the small remaining space at the end of the pew.

Hannah glanced at Cody but his eyes were focused on the organist, not her. She turned away, knowing she'd made a terrible mistake.

An hour later, after the congregation had sung "Silent

Night" by candlelight, most filed into the social hall for fellowship before heading home to spend Christmas Eve with their loved ones. An emptiness filled Hannah, not knowing where to go.

She realized the decision had been made for her when she saw Cody direct the girls toward the social hall with Nellie and Hank. He stood waiting in the aisle with his hands behind his back.

Hannah approached with caution, still trying to figure out how to explain her behavior.

But as usual, Cody's warm smile made it easy for her to relax.

"I'm glad you came." He spoke softly and extended his hand. "Would you like to go outside for a walk? There's a full moon."

Hannah accepted his hand and they headed to the door.

Outside, the air was brisk. Hannah inhaled a deep, calming breath. She longed for the stillness and serenity of this moment to remain with her forever. "It's beautiful out here." As far as Hannah could see, the snow-covered ground shimmered like a blanket of diamonds. The evergreen tree branches appeared coated with frosting.

"There's nothing better than taking a walk at night after a snowfall," Cody commented. Their footsteps made the occasional crunch. "Of course, usually I'm with Hershey." Cody stopped in his tracks and turned to face Hannah. "I'll admit, you're much better company."

Hannah smiled but avoided eye contact. Cody wasn't one to hold a grudge. He obviously was moving past their earlier text exchange. But still, he deserved an explanation.

Cody gently placed his hand under her chin. "Hey, are you okay? I hope you know you can talk to me...you don't have to be alone."

If she didn't tell him now, then when? "I got a job offer from my former school—in Phoenix," she blurted out.

The pristine white snow highlighted Cody's disappointment. "I see." He shoved his hands into the pockets of his wool dress coat. "Yesterday? The text from Lisa…is that what it was about?"

Hannah's words caught in her throat. She simply nodded.

"Have you accepted the position?" Cody stared at the ground.

"I'd be the principal of the school. It's an opportunity I'd be foolish to pass up." Speaking her response out loud did little to convince her it was the right thing to do.

Cody shook his head. "Yeah, I guess it would be a dream job for any teacher. Staying in a little town like Bluebell Canyon or having the opportunity to be in charge of a school in a big city…sounds like a no-brainer to me."

"They've given me until after the first of the year to decide." She looked away as unexpected tears burned at the backs of her eyes.

"I have a feeling you've already made the decision." Cody glanced toward the entrance of the church. "Right now, I've decided to go inside before everyone eats all of Nellie's brownies." He turned his attention back to her. "You're welcome to come with me."

Cody was only offering because he was kindhearted and it was what he was supposed to do. It wasn't what he really wanted. Hannah knew that. "No, you go on. Be with your family. I think I'm going to head home."

"Merry Christmas, Hannah."

The illuminating full moon disappeared behind a drifting cloud, leaving Hannah in darkness. She watched Cody step inside of the church. "Merry Christmas, Cody," she whispered to herself.

Chapter Sixteen

"Hey, you look like you could use another cup of coffee. Let's go in the kitchen," Logan leaned over and whispered to Cody.

"Sounds good." Cody peeled himself off the sofa at Logan and Caitlyn's house. For the past hour, the kids were busy opening Christmas gifts. Jake and his family were still at home nursing the stomach bug.

Cody took a seat at the kitchen table while Logan refilled their cups.

"What's up with you, man? You look like you lost your best friend out there. It's Christmas...you can't be walking around looking like Scrooge." Logan settled into the chair across from Cody and passed the steaming beverage.

I got a job offer from my former school.

Since Cody left Hannah standing outside of the church, the words hadn't stopped replaying over in his mind. "Hannah's leaving Bluebell Canyon." Cody struggled to speak the fact. Voicing the situation out loud made it even more of a reality.

Logan jerked his head back. "What are you talking about?" He grabbed Cody's forearm. "Tell me what's going on."

Over the next twenty minutes the brothers remained at the table. Once Cody told Logan about Hannah's job offer, he went on to recap the time spent with Hannah before spilling his guts. He explained to Logan how time spent with Hannah had played a role in his decision to go forward with legally adopting McKenzie and Madison. In the end, he confessed to his brother that he'd fallen in love with Hannah and hoped one day they could be a family.

"You can't let her go."

Cody ran his fingers through his hair. "What am I supposed to do? Ask her to give up her dream of becoming a principal for me? For some guy she's only known for two months?" He couldn't do that, especially after all of the heartache Hannah had experienced the past year.

"Forget about time. You said you love her, right?"

That was the one thing Cody knew for sure. "Honestly, I can't imagine my life without her."

"Then you've got to tell her. Give her a reason to stay."

Cody valued his younger brother's opinion, yet the sinking feeling in his stomach only filled him with more questions. "What if she says no?"

"But what if she says yes?" Logan's chair screeched across the hardwood floor as he stood and walked around the table. He rested his hand on Cody's shoulder. "Sometimes it's worth taking a chance."

Logan left the kitchen, leaving Cody alone with his thoughts and playing the *what if* game. He'd taken a chance with Mallory and look how that ended. She'd broken his heart. But Hannah wasn't Mallory. Hannah and his ex-girlfriend had nothing in common. How could he allow Hannah to go back to Phoenix without being completely honest with her about his feelings? As he recalled the night of their first kiss—believing it was only the first of many to come—he pushed away from the table.

"Girls, stay here and mind Uncle Logan and Aunt Caitlyn. I'll be back in a little while and then we'll head to the Garrisons' house," Cody announced while grabbing his coat from the hall closet.

"Where are you going?" Madison poked her head up from the gifts scattered across the floor.

As Cody exited Logan's home, he heard McKenzie giggling Hannah's name and telling her sister she knew where he was going. Inside the car, Cody realized McKenzie had eavesdropped again. He couldn't worry about that now. Before he saw Hannah, he had one stop to make along the way.

In record time, Cody arrived at Hannah's house. He spotted her car in the driveway and his shoulders relaxed for a second. Perfect.

Cody unfastened his seat belt and stepped outside of his truck. He circled around to the passenger side and opened the door. "Come on, girl. Welcome to your new home."

Cody patted his thigh two times, coaxing Ellie to jump out of the truck. "Sit." The dog obeyed his command while Cody attached the leash to her collar.

They headed up the front steps leading to the house. Cody spotted movement in the window. Hannah must have heard his truck.

Before he rang the bell, the front door opened.

"Merry Christmas," Cody said, smiling.

"Ellie!" Hannah's face was like a lighthouse beacon. A far cry from the way she looked last night.

Hannah dropped to her knees and hugged the animal. Ellie ate up the attention, slathering Hannah's hand with wet kisses. Seconds later, Hannah looked up at Cody. "Merry Christmas. What are you two doing here?"

"Can we come inside and I'll explain?" Cody asked. He was sure Hannah could hear his heart rattling against his ribcage.

Hannah stood and motioned for Cody. "Sure, come in."

They moved into the family room. The Christmas tree was plugged in and soft carols streamed through the sound system. Cody's heart ached for Hannah. He couldn't imagine what it would feel like to spend Christmas Day without loved ones.

If everything went according to plan, she'd never spend another holiday alone.

"Would you like something to drink? Coffee or hot chocolate?" Hannah offered while running her fingers through Ellie's coat.

"No thanks. I don't want to spoil my appetite for Nellie's big dinner. You still want to go with us, don't you?"

An uncomfortable silence hung in the air.

Hannah's face was expressionless.

This couldn't be good. "Hannah? You're coming, aren't you?" Cody already knew the answer, but he wanted to hear it straight from Hannah.

She bit her lip. "I was going to send you a text. I think it's best if I stay home. I've called Nellie to let her know."

Her words stung. She'd made her decision. Hannah had accepted the position. "I see." Cody gave a slight nod. "Well, I'm not going to stay long. I wanted to drop off your Christmas gift."

Hannah's eyes glanced at his hands. One still held Ellie's leash and the other was empty.

"I didn't know we were exchanging gifts." Hannah's face flushed.

"No. I—" Cody struggled for the right words. He didn't have any…not anymore. He extended his hand holding the leash. "Merry Christmas, Hannah."

A curtain of brown hair fell forward as she looked down at his hand. Once she lifted her head there were tears streaming down her cheeks. "Ellie? She's my gift?"

Cody swallowed the lump in his throat and nodded. He wasn't prepared for Hannah's emotional reaction to his gift.

"I don't know what to say. You know how much I love her, but she's been trained to work as a service animal. Don't you have a handler in mind for her?"

"You're right, she has been trained and that's exactly what

Ellie will do—for you. She can help you to manage your panic attacks by providing a source of emotional grounding." Cody paused to explain. "Let's say you're out in public and you feel an attack coming on. You can simply pet Ellie to redirect your attention away from the attack." Cody gave her a knowing look. "I don't need to explain all of this to you. You assisted with her training. You're well aware of the valuable support Ellie can provide."

Hannah rubbed her eyes with the sleeve of her sweatshirt. "Yes, I am. That's what makes your gift all the more special." She stepped closer and opened her arms. They hugged for a second before she pulled away, leaving him feeling empty and alone.

"I don't know how I can ever thank you for such an incredible gift."

You've got to tell her.

His brother's words from earlier filled Cody's already crowded mind. As much as he wanted to ask Hannah to stay, something told him now wasn't the time. The last thing he wanted was for Hannah to feel he was using Ellie as a pawn to keep her in Bluebell Canyon. Besides, she was leaving. What would be the point? "I know you'll take good care of her. That's thanks enough. Merry Christmas, Hannah." He turned and walked out of the house.

Once inside his truck, Cody gripped the steering wheel until his knuckles turned white. He hit the ignition button and slowly placed his foot on the accelerator. Against his better judgment, he glanced in his rearview mirror. Hannah stood on the front porch with her arms wrapped around her waist. Ellie sat at her feet.

Cody pulled his eyes away when he approached a stop sign. A part of him wanted to turn his vehicle around, head back to Hannah's house and ask her to stay. But he couldn't stand in the way of her dream. He loved her too much for that. When he looked in the rearview mirror for a second time, she was gone.

Hannah sat behind her desk and drew in a calming breath. The first day back to school following the Christmas and New Year's break was always a challenge for the students and their teachers. Today was no different.

After her alarm had sounded at six o'clock that morning, Hannah had struggled to get out of bed. Of course, Ellie wanted no part in Hannah hiding under the covers and calling in sick. Ellie had jumped up in the bed and licked Hannah's face excessively until she finally peeled herself from the warm nest and took the dog outside for a walk.

Once at school, the children ran on a sugar high from too many holiday treats. It took Hannah twenty minutes to get her class settled down long enough to focus on their math lesson. Hannah assigned five problems for the class to work on while she attempted to get a handle on her New Year calendar.

Her students weren't the only ones struggling to focus. Since Cody's visit on Christmas Day, Hannah hadn't been able to think about anything else. He'd given her a life-changing gift and how did she thank him? By allowing him to believe she'd made her choice and accepted the job? But she hadn't made her decision.

Once she told him she wouldn't be attending Christmas dinner with him at the Garrisons', she realized she'd sealed her fate. As she'd stood on the porch with Ellie and watched him drive away, she knew she'd made a terrible mistake. But the damage had been done.

With the children busy solving their arithmetic problems, Hannah attempted to shake off thoughts of Cody and the regret consuming her. She opened her calendar. Her eyes zeroed in on the big red circle around Friday. A heaviness grew in her chest. The day she agreed to give her former school an answer. Would she accept their offer to become the new principal?

Hannah dropped her pen, folded her hands and scanned her classroom. Teaching was her passion. Creating a positive and engaging atmosphere inside of her classroom that inspired children to want to learn was one of Hannah's greatest joys. Would she feel the same after assuming the role of principal, or would the job be less hands-on than having her own classroom?

"Stop copying me, McKenzie!" Amber's voice broke the silence of the room.

The time apart during the holiday hadn't cooled the tension between McKenzie and Amber. Hannah had hoped the bickering was over, especially after their last brawl on the playground had resulted in a meeting with the families and the principal.

"I'm not copying you!" McKenzie wasted no time responding to Amber's accusation. "You were looking at mine!"

Hannah rose from the desk and approached the girls while the other students observed the dispute. "Please keep your voices down. Your classmates are trying to work."

"But she's the copycat, not me!" McKenzie's face was like an overripe tomato. She sprang from her chair and ripped Amber's paper off her desk.

"McKenzie—that's enough. Give Amber's assignment back and follow me outside."

Hannah's sharp tone caused the other children to immediately turn their attention back to their math problems.

McKenzie stomped her feet all the way out to the hall. She looked up at Hannah and folded her arms across her chest. "Why doesn't Amber have to come out, too?"

"Because you were the one causing the disruption to the room, not Amber," Hannah answered quietly.

"Amber is stupid!"

Hannah inhaled a deep breath and released. "We don't call one another stupid, at least not in my classroom."

"Maybe I don't want to be in your room!" McKenzie was as angry as a swarm of hornets who had their nest disturbed.

Hannah wondered where the sweet little girl who'd been so helpful during the Christmas festival had gone. McKenzie was so happy and polite during the festivities, but the child standing in front of her today was full of anger. Something obviously was bothering her and it wasn't Amber. She'd just been the closest target.

"You're just picking on me because you don't like my uncle anymore." McKenzie rolled her lower lip and turned her head away.

Hannah's shoulders stiffened. This was about Cody. Questions swirled in her head. Had Cody said something to the twins about her job offer in Phoenix? "First of all, I'm not picking on you. Your behavior in the classroom was unacceptable. We don't handle situations by having outbursts like you did with Amber."

"She started it. I wasn't copying her—whatever." McKenzie's lip pressed tightly together.

"Second, the reason I called you outside the class has nothing to do with your uncle. I'm not sure where you got the idea that he and I were no longer friends, but that isn't true."

McKenzie shrugged her shoulders. "But you dumped him. He wanted to take you to the Garrisons for Christmas dinner." She hesitated for a second. "Are you going to call him and tell him I'm in trouble?"

This was what McKenzie wanted. She was still playing matchmaker with the hopes of bringing her and Cody together. "As I've mentioned before, your uncle is a busy man. I don't think it's necessary to bother him with this. Let's go back inside and you can apologize to Amber."

Hannah placed her hand on McKenzie's shoulder and headed to the door.

McKenzie made a sudden stop and looked up at Hannah. "I'll go, but I'm not going to apologize."

"Go inside and finish your math problems." Hannah decided not to push it. McKenzie wanted to continue to get herself into more trouble. Hannah wasn't going to play that game. She'd send Cody a message during lunch and ask him to stop by after school. But given how she'd treated him, would he even be open to such a meeting?

By the time the closing bell rang that same day, Hannah's students were out of gas. Her decision to allow extra time outside during recess to expel their pent-up energy was a success. Back in the classroom, she'd been able to work her way through the day's lesson plan without any further interruptions from her students, but she wasn't able to get her mind off Cody. He hadn't responded to her text message, but she wasn't surprised.

Hannah remained at her desk while the students filed out of the room. As they'd done every day since she first took over the class, the children made a point of smiling and saying goodbye to their teacher. A few even thanked her for the extended recess. It was this time of day that made all of the challenges that went along with being an educator worth it. Could she really walk away? For what? More meetings and stress. Less one-on-one time with the students. Becoming a principal might be a dream for most teachers, but not for Hannah.

She bowed her head in thanks. God had provided the answer. He was the God of second chances and new beginnings. His fresh start for Hannah was here in Bluebell Canyon, as a teacher.

"Can I talk to you, Miss Simpson?"

Lost in thought, Hannah hadn't noticed McKenzie standing in the doorway. With her hands behind her back, she looked like her sweet self again, not the red-faced angry little girl from earlier in the day.

Hannah stood and approached McKenzie. "Of course. You know my door is always open to my students. Where's your sister?"

"She's out in the car with Aunt Caitlyn."

Hannah took the child's hand and guided her to the craft table by the window. "Let's sit here."

McKenzie took a seat. Hannah sat in the empty chair beside her. "What did you want to talk about?"

Silence filled the space. McKenzie gazed outside while biting her lower lip.

Hannah placed her hand on McKenzie's arm. "You know, you can talk to me about anything."

McKenzie turned to her with tears in her eyes. "I'm sorry for what I said earlier."

"You should be apologizing to Amber, not to me."

"No." McKenzie shook her head. "I already told Amber I was sorry—out on the playground."

Hannah smiled. "I'm happy to hear this, but why are you still upset if you and Amber settled your disagreement?"

"I didn't mean what I said…about not wanting to be in your class. You're the best teacher in the world. Please don't move away." McKenzie sprang from her chair and flung her arms around Hannah.

"Oh, sweetie." Hannah stroked the back of McKenzie's hair and held her tight while she cried uncontrollably. "Please don't cry."

McKenzie lifted her head away from Hannah's shoulder. "I heard Uncle Cody tell Uncle Logan he wanted us to be a family." With tears streaming down her face, she frowned at Hannah. "How could you leave us?"

Hannah's mind flooded with regret. She looked at the pain she had caused. If she hadn't allowed Cody to believe she'd already accepted the position in Phoenix, McKenzie wouldn't be heartbroken. "I'm not leaving."

The earlier frown on McKenzie's face vanished, replaced by a smile that reinforced Hannah's decision. "You're not?" McKenzie's eyes widened.

"You're not?" A deep voice echoed McKenzie's words, followed by the sound of heavy boots slowly moving through the doorway. Hannah's insides vibrated when she spotted Cody.

McKenzie crawled off Hannah's lap, giving her the freedom to stand.

Breathless, Hannah stood frozen while Cody closed the space between them. His hazel eyes never left her own while he waited for her to answer.

"No, I'm not leaving. I've decided to stay and find out what God has in store for us."

Cody smiled and pulled Hannah into his arms. "That sounds like a good plan to me." He spoke softly, and his mouth moved closer to hers.

Hannah wrapped her arms around his neck and they kissed.

"Look McKenzie!" Madison raced into the classroom. Her snow boots skidded to a screeching stop beside her sister.

Smiling from ear to ear, McKenzie grabbed Madison's hands, unable to contain her joy. "Our plan worked!" The girls jumped up and down in celebration.

Before Hannah knew what was happening, Cody scooped her off her feet. Laughing, he spun her around and kissed her a second time. "Boy, did it ever."

Epilogue

Fourteen months later

Hannah covered her mouth with her hand and read the text message for a second time.

Out for delivery.

Today was the day.

"Come on, girl. Let's go up to the house and share the good news." Hannah patted her palm against the side of her thigh.

Ellie jumped to her feet and licked Hannah's hand. Over the past year, thanks to Ellie along with God's goodness, Hannah's panic attacks had subsided.

Hannah closed the door to her writing office and crossed the grassy field to the main house. She treasured her writing space, built by Cody as an engagement gift. He liked to call it her She Shed, but Hannah preferred Hannah's Hideaway.

Thanks to Cody, Hannah had a quiet place to abandon her unfinished book and begin work on something closer to her heart. Upon completion, she'd entered the manuscript in a contest sponsored by a prominent publishing house. When she received a call from an editor in New York that she'd won the contest and a book contract, she thought she was dreaming.

Marrying Cody and celebrating their union with their town

was the greatest blessing of all. It was Cody's idea to host the wedding reception at the exact location where they'd shared their first kiss only one year earlier. God was indeed a God of second chances.

Following Cody's proposal, the months leading up to the wedding ceremony passed quickly. During that time, Cody officially became McKenzie and Madison's father. And only two weeks ago, they'd celebrated another adoption. Hannah legally became the twins' mother. They were now one big, chaotic family, but Hannah wouldn't have it any other way. She loved her new life.

"We were just coming down to your office to bring you this." Cody flashed his gorgeous smile and moved toward her, carrying a box.

"I just got a delivery text." Hannah's heart pounded as she stepped inside of the kitchen.

"We know what it is, Mommy! We peeked at the label!" McKenzie danced across the floor.

"Girls, settle down. This is for your mother to open." Cody placed the box on the counter and handed Hannah a pair of scissors.

"My hand is shaking. Can you help me?" Hannah looked at Cody. Her eyes moistened with tears.

Cody cut away the packaging tape and slid the box closer to Hannah. "There you go."

"Hurry! Hurry! We want to see!" Madison grabbed her sister's hand and both bounced on their toes.

Hannah removed one of her books from the box. She closed her eyes and thanked God. "I can't believe I'm holding my first book."

Cody and the twins huddled closer.

"Hey, that looks like Ellie!" Madison pointed at the golden retriever on the front cover.

"But look at those girls—they're twins!" McKenzie shouted.

Cody took the book from Hannah's hand and pointed at the title. *Their Christmas Matchmakers.*

McKenzie's eyes widened with excitement. "That's us!" Her face looked like a chili pepper when she moved closer to Madison.

Cody scratched his head and turned to Hannah. "But you were already writing the book before we met?"

"Not this one. The manuscript I'd started long before we met was horrible, so I ditched it." Hannah took the book from Cody's hand and pressed it against her chest. "The three of you inspired me to write something from my heart—an unexpected second chance at love. The words poured out of me like never before. Thank you all for being my inspiration."

Cody gazed at Hannah. "So, I'm in the story, too?"

Hannah nodded, unable to speak.

"Why didn't I make the cover?" Cody joked and pulled Hannah into his arms. "I'm so proud of you."

"This is so cool! I can't wait to tell all of my friends," McKenzie said.

Cody removed another copy of the book from the box. "It looks like tonight I'll be reading my first romance novel. But can you sign my copy first?"

* * * * *

If you liked this story from Jill Weatherholt,
check out her previous Love Inspired books:

Searching for Home
A Dream of Family
A Home for Her Daughter
Their Inseparable Bond
Her Son's Faithful Companion

Available now from Love Inspired!
Find more great reads at www.LoveInspired.com.

Dear Reader,

Thank you for joining me once again in Bluebell Canyon!

The closer I got to writing the end of Cody and Hannah's story, I wished I'd given Cody more than three brothers! It was selfish of me, but I didn't want the series to end.

While developing Hannah's backstory, I couldn't help but think about all the trials we face in life. We all experience difficult times, some more than others. For Hannah, losing her husband and daughter in a tragic accident was one of her greatest and most painful trials she'd ever experienced.

But the good news is God never wastes hurt. He allows us to go through difficult situations in order for us to increase our dependence on Him. Even when things make little sense to us, God always has our best interest in mind.

I love to hear from readers, and I do my best to answer every email I receive. You can find me at jillweatherholt.com to sign up for my newsletter.

Blessings,
Jill